Man of Vision

The story of
Francis Worrell Stevens

by Helen Reardon

Man of Vision
Francis Worrell Stevens

New Zealand was a vibrant, changing country in the late 1800s and the story of my Stevens family is typical of life in the colony during those years. The major events in this story are based on true facts but the day to day lives of the characters come from the imagination of the writer.

1871 Chapter 1

"Francis, your father is up to his old tricks again." Ellen Stevens put down the newspaper and turned to face her husband who was using a telescope to look out over the bay.

"What is it this time my dear? Is he planning to intercept submarines or build another railway?"

"Neither. He now plans to patent a paddle wheel for propelling steamships. It is right here in today's paper."

Francis sighed. He had always lived in the shadow of his entrepreneurial father who was forever coming up with some scheme or other. The problem was he seldom had the finance to develop his ideas.

"I will telegraph my mother and hear her side of the story. She is well used to his ways and provides a healthy balance to their lives." He stood and walked across the room to where Ellen was sitting at the oval table with the day's newspaper spread out in front of her.

Ellen straightened her voluminous skirts and rang the bell beside her. "I will ask Maggie to send the children up ready for lunch. Young Clara would like to go to the beach this afternoon I am sure."

"I will accompany you, my dear. I would like to take the opportunity to get to know young Frank a little better." Francis was still getting used to the idea that his five-year-old son was now living with them full-time. Ellen had certainly taken on a burden when she agreed to marry him. Twice widowed, Francis was now responsible for his young son as well as the spirited Clara, the eight-year-old daughter from his first ill-fated marriage to Maria.

Clara had been brought up by her maternal grandparents in a country town south of Auckland but Ellen had insisted that she join them in Wellington where she could attend school and hopefully, learn to be a lady.

At that moment Clara bounced into the room, her skirts held high and her feet bare. "Will you please take me to the beach, Aunt Ellen? I will be ever so good for the rest of the day."

Ellen smiled at the child. It was just a short walk across the roughly paved road to the water's edge and the tide would be full. "Yes. We will all spend the afternoon on the beach and then walk along to Wilkinson's Tea Gardens for afternoon tea."

By now the young servant girl was placing food on the table and Francis began slicing the cold ham. Platters of fresh vegetables were arranged and thinly sliced bread set on the plates. Ellen served up a helping for young Frank, then the plates were handed around and everyone took a portion.

Francis smiled around at his family. His fortunes had certainly improved since he had met Ellen, the daughter of a southern landowner who had arrived from Ireland almost 20 years before. Ellen was merely a child when she first arrived in the new land, and the family had flourished as agriculture and land ownership made them a substantial fortune.

She had married a respected solicitor but he became ill and died just two years later, leaving her a widow. Francis was still reeling from the death of his second wife, Lydia, when they were introduced at a tea party held in the grounds of Government House.

Craving security, Ellen immediately set her sights on Francis Stevens and a short time later they were married in St Peter's Church at Te Aro, by the same minister who had officiated at his marriage to Lydia three years earlier.

Now, what had started as a marriage of convenience was working out well and Ellen was about to produce a child of their own.

"You must be happy that I persuaded you to build this lovely home right here at Oriental Bay. It will be a wonderful place to bring up our family." Ellen was right. A few fine homes were now scattered along the stony shores of the bay and although the road in front was rough and the land marshy, he could see a great future for the area.

"It has certainly been a good move for us and now you have bought the sections behind us, I feel that we have made a wise decision." Francis was still a little apprehensive at his wife's investment. At the time of her first marriage she had received a large sum of money from her father which had been wisely invested. Now after building the 14-roomed homestead, she had also bought several lots on the steep hillside behind them.

"We will be able to give the children a good start in life and that is important." Ellen was so thankful that she had been able to become pregnant as she was no longer a young woman. The child would be born in about three months' time and she would be proud to give Francis another healthy son.

The children were anxious to cross the road to the beach, but were instructed to rest for an hour to let their lunch settle. Ellen was pleased to put her feet up and Francis settled down to read the rest of the newspaper.

He re-read the news item again about his father. Every so often a story about Francis Worrell Stevens would appear. It was only three years ago that he had planned to build a railway, linking Nelson to the West Coast. He had been prepared to travel to London to raise the million pounds required, and he was willing to accept a large parcel of land in exchange for a railway.

Few railways existed in New Zealand at that time and the scheme had produced a great deal of criticism. While a venture in the province of Canterbury had been successful, the cost had bankrupted the Southland province. 'Far be it from me sir, to run down or throw cold water upon legitimate and honest undertakings, but when men without capital undertake to make railways to the moon, I think it is Moonshine. (Nelson Evening Mail, June 18, 1867)

When he had first arrived in New Zealand and worked in Auckland as a financier and stockbroker, Francis Worrell Stevens had applied for a patent to manufacture a machine for splitting shingles. Without sufficient backing, this scheme too had quietly disappeared.

Francis was thankful for his own steady job, working first in the Defence Office, then more latterly, as chief clerk in Crown Lands. He sat back in his chair and leaned back, his hands clasped behind his head. His mind went back to his arrival in New Zealand from England as a raw 19-year-old. His mother's brother, Samuel Vickers, had promised to find him employment, and he arrived just in time to join the Taranaki Rifle Volunteers who were involved with the first battles in the 1860 land wars.

After serving for 18 months with the rifle volunteers, he transferred to Auckland, working for the Commissariat stores where he was in charge of contracts between Auckland and the Waikato. With the transfer of the government to Wellington, the Auckland office merged with the Defence office and Francis and his young wife Maria were transferred to the capital city.

Francis sighed as he remembered the tragic death of his first wife just months after the transfer. She and two-year-old Ada had both been taken during the tragic scarlet fever epidemic that had raged around Wellington at the time. Three-month-old Clara had survived and was returned to her grandparents in Auckland and he lost touch with her for several years. She was a bright young thing and appeared to be adapting well to her new environment, even though Ellen was having trouble turning her into a young lady.

But there was no more time for day dreaming as the young people were ready to go to the beach and enjoy an afternoon in the sun. "Come along father, it's time to go." Young Frank was tugging his hand so he picked up his hat from the hall stand and made his way across the road with Ellen and Clara leading the way. Ellen had gathered together some towels and the children were already wearing their bathing suits.

They dodged the clumps of toi toi that grew in profusion along the beach and found a patch of clear sand where Ellen laid down a blanket and two folding chairs. "Now don't go out too far," she warned, as the children ran down to the water's edge and began splashing about.

"The children are getting along well considering they hardly know each other." Frank settled down in the chair, keeping an eye on his son and daughter. "I will always be grateful to you for making them welcome in our home."

"It will be even better when our own son is born." Ellen clutched her hands around her expanding form.

Francis was casting his eyes around the beach, taking in the rocky shore. "It would be good to see more sand on the beach. I will try to arrange for ballast from the cargo ships to be dumped here."

"That would be a great improvement. The beach is becoming quite popular and the tea gardens are attracting much attention." Ellen could see the day when large crowds would be attracted to the bay.

They sat for a while, occasionally chatting to other residents as they strolled by. Ellen was keen to be part of the Wellington social scene. Since arriving in the town she had found little time to make new friends but after her confinement she would make an effort to seek out suitable acquaintances.

"I think we should head for the tea gardens. The children would no doubt like some ice cream and a pot of tea would be most welcome." Francis got to his feet and called out to the children who were chasing crabs from their holes with long sticks. Leaving their blanket and seats on the front lawn of their house, they covered the children's bathing suits and made their way along the rough roadway to the very end of the beach. A row of small houses had been built against the steep cliff and larger homes were slowly appearing on the higher slopes.

A large steamer was making its way into the port, and a number of sailing craft were racing out on the bay. Today was calm but at times the wind that blew in from the strait was very strong, making the crossing from the South Island quite treacherous.

Ellen took Francis' arm as they walked over the rough surface. The track was only just wide enough for a horse and cart and she did not wish to risk a fall. The children, however, ran ahead and reached the tea gardens ahead of them.

"Come on father. The ice cream is waiting," Clara called. Ice cream from a tea shop was a real treat after living in the country for so many years.

"Be patient, young lady. We have all the time in the world." Francis caught up with the children as they waited in the colourful garden outside the tea rooms. He knew that it had all been created by a Scottish nurseryman named David Wilkinson who was one of the earliest settlers in the area.

Francis led the way into the spacious interior which was decorated in a grand manner and used as a meeting place by many local groups and societies. A waitress greeted them and they followed her to a table which overlooked the bay where Ellen ordered tea and an assortment of pastries and cakes and a cone of ice cream for each of the children.

Little Frank sat on the tall chair, his feet dangling in the air. Clara tried her best to act like a young lady but couldn't resist squirming around to take in the sights. The women were elegantly gowned and she looked down at the thin shift which had been pulled over her damp bathing costume.

Her hair was still wet from the sea and hung in a scraggy fashion around her shoulders. Her eyes lit up at the sight of the ice cream cone, however, and she and Frank were sent out to sit on the steps where they could enjoy the treat.

"Help yourself to one of these delicious pastries, my dear. They are reputed to be the best in the whole of Wellington." Francis took one of the cream-filled delights and tried to avoid getting the crumbs on his beard. He wiped his face with a linen napkin and took a mouthful of tea.

"This is certainly a pleasant way to spend an afternoon. We will have to make it a regular event." Ellen was enjoying the elegant surroundings and eyeing up the patrons for a possible friend. She still missed her sisters who had all remained in the South Island and was keen to find some suitable companions.

By now the children had finished their ice creams and Ellen wiped their faces and instructed them to sit down and choose a cake from the selection. The next few minutes passed peacefully as the family enjoyed the treat.

As they were about to leave a tall, sandy-haired man with a genial smile stopped beside their table and introduced himself as Captain James Jones. "I believe we are almost neighbours," he said. "I have lived for a time further along the parade and my wife and I would like to meet you and share some time together."

"That would be most pleasant." Francis introduced himself and Ellen and the children.

"Then why don't we make it next week. I will be in touch as soon as I have consulted my wife." Captain Jones shook Francis by the hand and returned to his seat.

Ellen felt a buzz of excitement. Their first invitation. It would be something to look forward to over the next few days.

Chapter 2

The city of Auckland was reeling at the latest scandal. A prominent stock broker, Herbert Stevens, who had worked with his father at the prestigious stock broking firm of Stevens and Sons had married a local lady and absconded on the ship Nebraska, which had set sail for San Francisco.

The only problem was that Herbert was already married, and the father of four young children, and he went through the marriage ceremony, using his brother Sydney's name.

By the time the residents of Auckland heard of the marriage, Herbert and his 18-year-old bride were out on the high seas, never to be heard of again.

"The bounder. It was less than a year ago that he left our partnership and he has been running his own affairs since then." Francis Worrell Stevens was mortified. "How dare he bring such discredit to our name."

"I can't believe our son would deceive us all in this manner. What were the young lady's parents thinking of to allow such a marriage to go ahead without meeting with us?" Barbara Stevens was inconsolable.

"The parents had to pass my office to get the marriage licence and it appears his neighbours could have told him that Herbert had a wife and four young children at Parnell." Francis Worrell was furious.

His wife laid her hand on his arm. "Calm down my dear. We will do our best to help Jane and the children and see that they are provided for."

Francis threw down the paper and walked out into the garden which overlooked Grafton gully. He sat on a wooden bench and held his head in his hands. The damage that this scandal could bring to their firm was hard to estimate.

The business was a precarious one and it was easy to lose the confidence of clients who were buying shares in land, houses and mining rights. Francis still owned considerable parcels of land in the various suburbs of Auckland, but his debt level was high.

"Come along Francis. There is no point in crying over spilt milk." Barbara Stevens was always the peace maker. She had been through good times and bad with her unpredictable husband, first while he was a school master, running a school near Epping Forest in Essex, and then living in grand style in London where he set up a stock broking and money lending business.

"We were practically down to our last penny when we arrived in New Zealand and you have done very well over recent years. I'm sure we will rise above this latest set back." Barbara was always confident.

Francis sat up and pulled himself together. Yes, they had done well in Auckland and the rest of his sons were fine, upstanding men who could hold their heads up high. Sydney continued to be a partner in the stock broking firm and Walter and Francis were both employed by the government and living in Wellington.

"I hope people will remember my generosity in giving land on the North Shore for the new church and parsonage to be built. I still have the grateful reply from the Bishop of New Zealand, acknowledging the gift."

With that, Francis stood and took his wife in his arms. "I am so grateful for your loyalty through all these years. I will saddle my horse and ride into town as though nothing has happened."

Barbara sat on the seat and sighed. Her life in New Zealand was certainly different from her early days in London where her father Joseph Vickers had owned a theatre. When her brother Samuel moved to New Zealand and her husband's London business was in dire straits, the family decided to follow Samuel and try their luck in the new colony.

She could look back on the last 40 years without one day of regret, even though their fortunes had soared and plummeted several times. They had plenty to be thankful for and the action of their third son was not going to destroy them.

But now there was no time to waste. She would need to write letters to Francis and Walter in Wellington and share the news. Dear Walter had married Emily Boughton, whose father was an old friend from the London Stock Exchange. They had been so happy when their son Charles was born just over a year ago.

As for Francis, after so much heart break he seemed happy enough with Ellen, and was settling down with his family in their new home in Oriental Bay. Soon there would be another child to welcome and she was looking forward to making the sea journey to Wellington when the baby was born.

Sydney was now the only son working for the family firm and he was mainly based in Grahamtown where the mining shares for the Thames gold fields were being sold. Sydney would be horrified to have his name linked to the fraudulent marriage, Barbara realized.

"I really must contact him as soon as possible," she said to herself, as she pulled out the paper and pen from her writing desk. Writing all those letters would take her the best part of the afternoon.

As Francis rode towards the business centre he looked around at the developing town. Much of the timber had been milled and small holdings were dotted along the route. A deep gully was now fringed with houses built to take advantage of the magnificent view of the harbour and off-shore islands.

The Stevens were fortunate to be leasing a plot of land and a large wooden home built for a sea captain. A gardener was employed to care for the grounds and Barbara had found a capable woman to manage the household.

Yes, for the moment life was treating them well but this latest scandal was most unwelcome. It didn't take much to shake the confidence of investors and Francis knew that with such a large debt and money outstanding they could be on shaky ground.

He urged his mount into a canter as they came to a stretch of grassland then gathered him together as they reached the outskirts of Auckland town. He had recently moved his business into premises in Queen Street which dropped steeply down to the waterfront. Many substantial buildings now lined the street and a wide variety of business houses were flourishing.

Reaching his premises, Francis let his horse loose in the small field behind the building and unlocked the door. His son Sydney was in Grahamtown for the rest of the week but would no doubt want to return to Auckland to disassociate himself from the affairs of his brother.

Francis suspected that there would be many people left out of pocket by Herbert's sudden departure and were likely to call on him to try to make good their losses. He knew that Barbara's brother Samuel Vickers would also be most upset by the news.

He settled at his desk and leafed through some papers as he waited for the onslaught. In fact, it was just moments later that his brother-in-law bustled into the room.

"Young Herbert has left us in a grave predicament," he said. "We must enter his office and search through his paper work. Goodness knows what sort of mess he has left behind."

"I agree. Hopefully his secretary will still be working in the building and will allow us access to his ledgers." Francis folded his glasses into their case and prepared to follow Samuel to the office which Herbert had occupied, just a few doors away.

A large notice had been pasted on the bolted door. 'Closed until further notice' it read.

The two men stared at the note in consternation. They knew that although Herbert was no longer a partner in the firm of Stevens and Son, his sudden departure could bring disrepute to the name.

"I will place an advertisement in the newspaper disclaiming any connection with my son." Francis face had paled at the sight of the closed building.

"That sounds like a wise move and in the meantime we must consult our lawyer and see what can be done to minimize the damage. I am most sorry for my sister and yourself." Samuel patted Francis on the arm as he headed to where his horse was tied to the hitching rail. He rode away with a grim look on his face. It was through his influence that the Stevens family had come to New Zealand and he often felt responsible for their well-being.

Francis walked a little further down the street until he came to the news agent's office. He sat at a desk and proceeded to draught out a notice. 'Herbert Stevens has no business connection with the firm of Stevens and Son, share brokers, nor has he had since January 1870. Signed, Francis W Stevens, Sydney Stevens.'

The clerk took the paper and looked at it with interest but made no comment. "Thank you Mr Stevens. This notice will appear in tomorrow's paper and an amount will be charged to your account."

He had already handled a number of press releases that day, all relating to the illegal marriage and subsequent disappearance of Herbert Stevens. After dealing with routine paperwork most of the time, a little bit of scandal was sparking up his day. He must inform his editor of the possibility of an interesting story.

Soon Francis was back in his office. He would try to contact Herbert's secretary and get access to his son's premises. He knew the woman lived in a boarding house within walking distance of Queen Street and would call there later in the day.

The rest of the afternoon passed quickly. A number of anxious gentlemen put their heads in the door to enquire about Herbert's whereabouts. They had seen the notice on the building but had obviously not caught up with the news that Herbert had left on the ship.

Francis did his best to placate them and offered to look up the records to ascertain whether their investments were safe. With any luck he might gain some new clients out of this sorry affair.

It was late afternoon when he packed up his paperwork and prepared to leave the office. Who knew what tomorrow would bring? Hopefully the situation would resolve itself before the week was over.

Chapter 3

With two days to go, Ellen Stevens was looking forward to the invitation to Captain Jones residence. She had passed the palatial home many times on the way to town and often wondered who lived there. Like most of the houses in the bay the two-storied dwelling was built from Kauri timber with Victorian decoration and a low picket fence along the front.

With her pregnancy so advanced, it was difficult to find a suitable dress to wear but she settled on a soft flowing style in grey silk. Her two-strand pearl necklace and matching ear rings would look well enough along with a number of elaborate rings on her fingers.

Francis was looking forward to learning more about their host and his family. He knew that James Jones was captain of the ferry which ran between the port area and Eastbourne. He was reputed to be a genial man who was very popular with his passengers.

Clara was also full of excitement as the children had been invited to tea along with their father and Ellen. She would wear her new dress of embroidered silk with matching slippers and her hair was to be curled with hot tongs. Young Frank was more interested in meeting the captain and hearing stories about life on the sea.

When Francis returned from work that evening on the horse-drawn tram he was carrying a folded newspaper under his arm. His face looked concerned as he greeted his wife and hugged the children.

"It seems my family cannot keep out of the news. I can hardly believe what my young brother has done." He flung himself into a chair and handed the paper to Ellen.

"What is it my dear? Not bad news I hope." Ellen looked at her husband with concern and quickly scanned the pages.

The headline caught her eye. 'Stockbroker absconds with young lady'. "That is surely not true. Herbert is married to a very honorable woman and their fourth child was born less than a year ago."

"Read the rest of the story. It just gets worse. Herbert married in the name of my brother Sydney and has left on a boat for America. If he owes money I hate to think what sort of problems my father will have to face." Francis sighed. His father's financial state was often precarious and a scandal like this could be his undoing.

They were startled by the sound of the door bell ringing and soon Walter Stevens was being shown into the room. He held a copy of the newspaper out to Francis and sunk into the nearest chair.

"My wife will be horrified as Herbert's latest child is even younger than our son. With four small children and no income, how will Jane manage?"

Ellen sat and listened to the two men. She was furious that Herbert should let the family down in such a way. "Jane was given a large tract of land by her father and has a supportive family who will help her I am sure. I am more concerned about the harm this will do to your father's reputation as a stock broker. If it wasn't for the gold mining shares, they would already be in deep trouble."

Walter knew full well of the problems ahead. At one time he had also worked for his father in Auckland but had accepted a position with the Treasury and moved to Wellington when the government shifted there in 1865.

He and his wife Emily enjoyed a comfortable lifestyle in the capital city, although it had taken three years before a live child was born. Now little Charles was the apple of his eye and his marriage to Emily was a happy one.

"I'd better be off. We will keep in touch and try to help our father in the best way we can." Walter left as quietly as he had arrived.

"I will keep away from the town for the next few days until the scandal has died down. I hope this will not spoil our invitation to the Jones' residence on Saturday." Ellen would hate to miss out on the only invitation they had received in a long time. She was desperate to be part of the Wellington social scene and anxious to make a good impression on their hosts.

In spite of her pregnancy her mind was always working and she already had plans to build new houses on the Hay Street allotments which she had bought. The street had been named as part of the 1840 NZ Company street plan and although it was merely a dirt track she could visualise a number of fine homes with views over the harbour.

She had recently been in touch with a builder of her choice and asked him to plan the next house a little way up the hill. It would be a two-storied wooden building with great rental potential. Every merchant in the town would want to live in this quiet waterfront community. While Francis was fretting about the fortunes of his father she was already planning a future for themselves.

The papers over the next two days were full of the scandal and by the time Saturday came along Francis and Ellen were a little nervous about their reception at the Jones' household. What if their hosts thought badly of them?

When the time came they dressed carefully and walked the short distance to the captain's home. On their arrival the greetings were warm and the children were welcomed and taken to the nursery where James' children were waiting to greet them.

With two children and another on the way the captain's wife was most charming. "Come my dears, and share the activities while your parents relax and enjoy a drink before dinner."

Clara was a little nervous but when she found that she was the eldest she was soon organizing the younger children as they played. There was a small boy the same age as Frank and a little girl of three and before you knew it they were enjoying a variety of games and toys and the sound of laughter rang out.

Soon they were summoned to the dining room where the adults were ready for the meal. Clara couldn't help giggling as they took their seats at a small table at one end of the room. Her slippers had come off and her newly curled hair was a tangled mess.

Ellen scowled but the captain's wife smiled in her direction. The captain said grace and the light meal was served. Francis was enjoying the company of the Welsh captain who entertained with accounts of life on the sea. Mind you, most of his experience was on the short route across to Eastbourne but nevertheless the stories flowed.

There was no mention of the scandal in Auckland. Either the connection hadn't been made or the Jones family was too polite to mention it. Ellen was relieved and soon relaxed in the company of Esther Jones. Their babies were due around the same time and they were soon comparing notes and sharing advice.

"I have a doctor booked as it is my first time," Ellen said. "I am no longer a young woman so my husband and I were very relieved when I became pregnant."

"The local midwife is very good. I think I will be in safe hands," Esther smiled. She realized that Ellen was not the mother of Francis' two children and was anxious to learn more about the situation. Young Clara was a lively child and little Frank a little more subdued.

When she realized that Clara had been raised in the country she made an offer that took Ellen by surprise. "We have a small pony in our field that we bought for our eldest child. He is not able to manage it on his own, so perhaps Clara would like to ride it from time to time."

"I'm sure she would love to. It is one of the things she has missed since coming to live in Wellington. That is most kind of you." Ellen was sure that Clara would be overjoyed at the prospect but she would talk it over with Francis first.

Chapter 4

It was three weeks later that little William Stevens was born. Ellen had been admitted to the cottage hospital two days earlier and at two in the morning the baby came into the world after a difficult labour.

Francis looked at his wife with concern as he stood at her bedside. She was exhausted and he was fearful as he had already lost two wives following childbirth.

"Never again Francis. That was an ordeal I don't want to repeat." Ellen closed her eyes and turned away from her husband trying to forget the excruciating pain she had experienced as the child was born.

"Don't worry, Mr Stevens. "Most women have the same reaction just after they have given birth. The memories soon fade when they hold the child in their arms." The nurse was used to such scenes, especially from a first-time mother.

Francis watched her straighten the bed covers and pull the curtains closed around the bed. He followed the woman to the nursery where the babies lay in identical cots. When she picked little William up and held him, Francis could see his son through the glass. Yes, he was a fine, healthy child and he knew Ellen would be proud to be his mother.

Now it was time to return home where the children would be waking up to the news of their new brother. The servant girl Maggie had been asked to oversee the children during the night while Francis waited at the hospital but he would have to make sure they had breakfast and Clara was ready for school.

He had taken a few days' leave from his job so had the time to escort Clara to the cab and then it would be up to him to entertain his son for the rest of the day. Maybe Frank would like to ride into town in the carriage and buy something for his new brother.

Francis was pleased that the news of his brother's disgraceful conduct was no longer making headlines in the newspapers. It had been a difficult three weeks and he wondered how his parents were faring in Auckland. He had received the note from his mother giving more details about the fraudulent marriage but knew it was not practical for him to make the long journey to Auckland to check out the situation.

Clara was already out of bed by the time he returned to Oriental Bay. Her face lit up as he told her about her new brother. A nursery had been prepared for him and she opened the door and looked at the piles of small garments and the stuffed toys which decorated the room.

"Frank will be pleased to have a little brother and I am happy that Aunt Ellen is well." She picked up a blue bear and laid it in the frilled cot. "I'm sure little William will like the bear. It will be his first friend."

Francis smiled. He was exhausted as he had been awake most of the night, but knew there would be a big welcome for his small son when he was old enough to be brought home. "Come now, we will see if breakfast is ready and I will take you to meet the cab."

As the day went on, Francis rested for a time, then asked the groundsman to prepare the horse and carriage for the ride into town. With little Frank beside him he drove along the parade and around the corner towards Courtney Place.

Several boat sheds had been built haphazardly along the edge of the bay and a number of small craft were tied to their buoys out in the harbour.

The town had grown rapidly since the government was moved from Auckland and businesses were importing goods and setting up stores to tempt the increasing population.   Francis thought of the ambitious public works programme recently suggested by politician Julius Vogel who proposed to borrow several million pounds from the London money markets to fund the building of roads, public buildings and port facilities as well as more than a thousand miles of railway.

He smiled as he recalled his father's plan to do exactly the same thing just a few years before. The policy hinged on the cheap acquisition of Maori land, but building a railway across a mountainous, geologically unstable country would require massive borrowing as well as an assisted immigration programme to provide the labour.

It was ironic that his father Francis Worrell Stevens was always ahead of his time, then someone else would come along a few years later with the same idea.

By now they had arrived in Cuba Street and pulled up outside the premises of Thompson's drapery store. Perhaps young Frank could purchase his gift to his new brother here. They tied the horse to the hitching rail and went inside. Shop assistants stood behind the long wooden counters and all manner of goods were piled on the shelves behind them.

Francis asked to see some small boys' clothing and Frank looked around for a toy he could buy. He spied a large rocking horse but Francis shook his head and pointed him towards a display of wooden toys. A brightly coloured wagon which could be pulled along by a string took his eye and this was soon wrapped, along with a small blue coat.

"We will write your names on the card and you and Clara can give them to Ellen when she comes home. She will be delighted, I am sure." Francis paid for his purchases and left the store, his little son clutching the package.

They returned to the carriage and drove along the waterfront to where the coastal steamers were anchored. Men were unloading the goods onto carts and Frank was fascinated by the busy scene.

Soon it was time to make their way back to Oriental Bay and the tranquility of the gentle waves lapping against the rocks.

"This bay is a piece of paradise, my son, and no-one must be allowed to take it away from us." Francis turned into their gateway and handed the horse over to the young lad who helped the groundsman. "Thank you. See that the horse is fed and watered. I will need him again later in the day."

It was late afternoon before Francis mounted the horse and rode in the direction of the hospital. He was anxious to see Ellen and check on her well being. She should be feeling more rested by now and in a better humour.

When he walked into the room he was surprised to see her sitting up in bed and the room decorated with flowers and cards. "Look at this Francis. So many people have already sent their good wishes. Our son is well and I have already given him his first feed."

Ellen was positively glowing as Francis gave her a hasty kiss and sat on the chair beside the bed. "I am pleased that you are feeling so much better, my dear and thank you for giving me a healthy child."

He filled Ellen in on the events of the day and they sat together for the allotted hour. "I will look in at the nursery on the way out. Have a good rest and I will see you at the same time tomorrow."

Francis lined up at the nursery window with the other new fathers and admired his son from afar. The men all seemed a trifle embarrassed but shook each other by the hand before they went on their way.

By the time he got home Clara was anxious to visit the Jones' household to have her first ride on the pony she had been offered. She wore her riding outfit and was impatient to be on her way. "I feel that I must rest, Clara, but I will let Maggie accompany you. I'm sure she is an experienced horse woman."

Young Maggie was only too happy to leave her indoor duties to visit the Jones' household. She had her eye on the young man they employed and this was a great opportunity to get to know him better.

"Come along then Clara. We will soon get the better of the spoilt pony I am sure." She grabbed her coat and sturdy shoes and soon the pair were racing off along the road to where the small pony was kept in a yard beside the house.

A tall young man came out from the shed and smiled shyly at Maggie. He went into the stable and came back out with a bridle and saddle and helped Clara put the bit in the pony's mouth. "He always tries to nip you so keep away from his teeth if you can," he said. "He is quite a naughty little animal."

Clara laughed. She was well used to handling horses of all sizes and knew she would soon have the small pony eating out of her hand. "What is his name?" she asked. "It's Whiskey as he is black and white, and by the way, my name is George." He addressed this remark to Maggie who blushed and stood to one side.

Soon the pony was saddled and the girth pulled tight. George opened the gate and led him around the small field for a few minutes, then tightened the girth again.

"Okay. He should be ready now." He hoisted Clara onto the saddle and handed her the reins. She adjusted the stirrups and sat up straight.

"Okay Whiskey, let's see what you can do." The pony was reluctant to leave the yard but after a sharp kick from Clara he moved away and began circling the field. Soon he was urged into a trot and then a canter as he returned to where Maggie and George were standing.

By this time, Eleanor Jones had noticed what was going on and came out to join them. "That was very good, my dear child. You really are an accomplished rider. You are most welcome to come here and ride Whiskey at any time. He needs the exercise or he will get too fat." She patted the pony on the neck, pleased to have found someone capable of riding him until her own son was old enough to manage on his own.

Clara spent the next half hour riding Whiskey around the field. It felt so good to be back on a pony again. She had been riding as long as she could remember back on the farm with her grandparents. It seemed that life in Wellington was about to get a lot better.

It was a whole week before Ellen and baby William were allowed home. Francis had hired a part-time nurse to help with the child and Ellen was grateful for the assistance. The baby was feeding well and seemed content but it was good to have the assurance that all was well.

She had been shown how to bathe and dress the child but she never seemed to get enough sleep. The baby woke during the night and again early in the morning and Ellen wondered how other mothers coped, especially if they had no help. Clara loved to hold little William and Frank showed him toys and talked to him.

"I will be pleased to get back to work for a rest," Francis laughed at the busy scene. He knew there would be plenty to keep him occupied back in the Crown Land office where he now worked. Land would need to be set aside for the proposed roads and railway lines and every province was urging government to build railways to serve their areas.

"The British settlers used the railway back home and expect the same service here. Public demand is getting very strong."

Ellen sighed. She knew that the building of a railway had bankrupted her province of Southland and she had little faith in the project. "The new arrivals will just have to get used to our ways," she said. "If they don't like it they can go back to where they came from."

"I'm sure you would appreciate rail travel if it was available. Imagine being able to go overland to Auckland instead of the uncomfortable journey along the coast." Francis knew that the railway would be the making of the country as the existing roads were little more than tracks over steep and mountainous terrain.

"You are right my dear, but I hope the debt will not overburden our government." Ellen was a cautious investor and not likely to risk her funds on an uncertain venture.

But now it was time for Clara to go riding and Francis had promised to accompany her. He was keen to see how she was coping with the wayward pony and pay his respects to the owner. Mrs Jones' baby was due any time and Ellen would like her to call and share afternoon tea before the event.

"Be sure to give Eleanor the invitation. I'm sure she would like to see our beautiful new son." Ellen was anxious to get better acquainted with their neighbour. She was tired of being confined to the house and ready for company.

"I'll give her the message, now go and rest while you have the chance." Francis set off with the children in tow leaving Ellen to enjoy a quiet hour before the baby was due to be fed.

Chapter 5

Francis Worrell Stevens was about to close the office for the day when his son Sydney pulled his horse up outside and tied it to the hitching rail.

"Father, I have finally had time to come to Auckland. It has taken me three days to ride here."

"Sydney, my son, do come in. So much has happened since I last spoke to you and I saw your notice in the newspaper a short time ago stating that you were not married to Miss Paul. What a state of affairs!"

Sydney sat down in the sturdy wooden chair beside the desk. "Were you and our lawyers able to minimize the damage to our business?"

"It hasn't been as bad as I thought it would be but Herbert left owing a considerable amount of money. He had sold mining shares which belonged to his clients and they haven't received a penny of it. Luckily, most people realise that we are not to blame, but business has definitely slowed down as a result."

Sydney was thoughtful. "The share broking business is not as lucrative as it once was. Most of the big projects are now being financed by the government's new public works programme and the demand for gold mining shares is slowing down."

"Is the Thames gold field still producing? The towns of Shortland and Grahamstown are booming I believe."

"The gold boom is fading. There is much gold still in the hills but it is becoming more difficult to extract. In fact, I have been considering moving back into the post and telegraph department where there would be a more secure future." Sydney had commenced working for the department when he left school and he had always been tempted to return.

"It sounds as though you are ready to desert the sinking ship. I would be sorry to see you go, but as you say, there may not be enough work for the two of us if the mining is slowing down." Francis was upset that his son would consider leaving him but knew that he had to secure his own future.

"I have been offered a position as chief clerk at Timaru in the South Island. It is about as far away as you can go but with the telegraph network soon to be extended across the country I feel that it would provide secure employment." Sydney had been dreading this conversation with his father. For some time he had realised that their business was far from secure and he had been planning to move on."

"It would be a sad day if you left the firm but you know your mother and I will support any decision you make." Francis looked sadly at his son. He could see that he had already made up his mind to take the job in Timaru.

"Come, I will buy you a drink at the club before we go home. I suppose you will be staying at your lodgings for the time being."

"I may as well. There will be several loose ends for me to tie up before I leave, but I have completed my work at Grahamstown. The clerk there is capable of keeping the office open for a time." Sydney had been busy handing over his work to the capable man, but there was work to be completed at the Auckland office.

The two men mounted their horses and rode the short distance to the Auckland Club which had been opened to cater for gentlemen like themselves. They would enjoy a drink or two in convivial surroundings before making their way home.

Back at their home in Grafton, Barbara was excited at the news of the birth of William Stevens in Wellington. The announcement had appeared in the newspapers a short time before but communication was difficult and letters took many days to reach their destination.

She would dearly love to travel to Wellington to see her new grandson. They had been unable to attend the wedding of Francis and Ellen and she had not visited the new home in Oriental Bay or caught up with the older children since they were babies.

When Francis finally arrived home from the club she told him of her desire to make the journey on the coastal steamer. Francis was in a sombre mood as he shared the news of their son's decision to leave the business.

However, he was eager to please his wife. Who knew what was in store for them?

"If you feel the need to go to Wellington I will arrange your ticket. My friend Alexander McGregor has recently launched a new steam ship which will take you as far as Napier in the Bay of Plenty, then you will need to transfer to another vessel to take you the rest of the way." Francis knew that the trip to Wellington would be a difficult one but he could use his influence to obtain a comfortable cabin for his wife. After all, he was a member of the syndicate of businessmen which supported Captain McGregor.

Barbara was overjoyed. She was looking forward to seeing her new grandson as well as the rest of Francis' family and getting to know her daughter-in-law whom she had never met.

"Thank you dear Francis. You make me so happy." She gave Francis a warm kiss and began to plan the visit.

It took a week to make the arrangements and as Barbara left the Auckland pier she was grateful that her husband had been able to arrange the ticket and transport her to the wharf. The steamer was small and the accommodation simple, but comfortable. They would call at several settlements along the way and she knew she would be relieved when she reached the capital town.

She went below to find her berth and luckily she had a cabin to herself. The journey would take several days but she would be comfortable and well fed. She recalled arriving in New Zealand many years before with her husband and several children. After many months at sea she knew that her brother Samuel would be waiting to welcome them but the long journey had taken its toll.

Barbara hung her clothing in the narrow cupboard then made her way to the lounge area where several of the other passengers had gathered. The men were seated at one end of a long table while a small cluster of women sat in the comfortable chairs in front of the port holes.

"Come and join us my dear." An elderly woman in a fashionable gown beckoned to Barbara in a friendly manner. "If we are to endure this journey we may as well do it in comfort."

Barbara smiled and took the seat on offer. A porter appeared with a tray of drinks and she took a small glass of sherry which she sipped appreciatively. This was a lot more civilized than being bounced around in a carriage over bumpy roads.

The steamer had made its way out of the harbour, and was headed south towards the Coromandel Peninsula. As it reached open water the sails were unfurled and the ship sped along across the smooth water, making good time in spite of its heavy load of cargo and coal.

It wasn't long before the 50 passengers were summoned to the dining room where an excellent dinner was served. The glasses were refilled and the conversation became spirited. Once again Barbara was seated with the few women who were travelling alone.

Through the port holes they could see the Coromandel ranges in the distance and knew they would anchor in the small harbour early next day. A few passengers would disembark and cargo unloaded, mostly supplies for the gold miners who were still seeking their fortunes.

Barbara was ready to retire early and settled on the narrow bunk where she soon fell asleep in spite of the sounds of the sea and the creaking of the ship. She was wakened in the early hours, however, by the sound of the engine which had been fired up ready to make the run into the harbour.

She decided to wash and use the toilet which was behind a door at one side of her cabin. With the rocking of the boat it was difficult to dress in her many garments but she did the best she could and was soon ready to walk on the deck to enjoy the view of the rugged coast line.

A number of passengers, well wrapped up against the cool breeze, were already standing at the ship's rail and there was great excitement when a school of dolphins was sighted. They leapt from the water right beside the ship and followed the craft for some time before heading of in a different direction.

Barbara could see the settlements of Grahamstown and Shortland in the distance. She imagined her son Sydney hard at work in the waterfront office. Francis had not informed her of his return to Auckland. He would give her the news on her return.

Barbara was ready for the tasty breakfast which was being served in the dining room and sat at one of the tables waiting to be served. A young woman handed her a menu and she chose a hearty meal of sausage, eggs and potato as well as toast and a cup of tea.

"Thank you lass." She smiled at the young woman who served her, judging her to be freshly arrived from Britain. "Where are you from?" she asked.

"Liverpool, madam. I have been in this country just over a month and was fortunate to find employment so quickly."

"You are certainly seeing much of your new land. The best of luck to you."

Barbara couldn't help admiring the courage of such a young person to venture into the new world. She ate her meal in silence then returned to her cabin for a short nap before the ship anchored at Coromandel.

The next two days went by smoothly until they passed the port of Tauranga and were rounding the East Cape and heading for their destination of Napier. A sudden storm came up and the small ship was tossed about like a cork on the water. Although they were always in sight of land, Barbara was becoming increasingly nervous.

She had experienced wild conditions before but that had been on a much larger vessel. She hoped the small craft was capable of coping with such high seas. A porter knocked on the cabin door to enquire whether she was all right and suggested she go up into the lounge area where she would be more comfortable.

Barbara agreed and clutching the porter's arm she mounted the wooden staircase that led to the upper deck. She landed with a thud in one of the seats and sat upright, gripping the arms of the chair as the sea rose and fell.

Mercifully, once the ship rounded the coast, conditions improved and everyone relaxed, knowing that the worst was over.

"I'll be glad when the railway line is built. It will be much more pleasant to travel by train." A young man was seated beside Barbara and she agreed. She told him of her husband's plan to build a railway in the South Island, from Nelson to the West Coast.

"Unfortunately the province didn't agree at the time and now I believe a railway network is planned for many parts of the country."

"Indeed. In fact I am travelling to Wellington to promote the idea for the Auckland province. Railway is the only answer to opening up such a rugged country."

"You will probably meet one or other of my sons who work for the government in Wellington. Francis is involved in land acquisition and Walter works in the Treasury." Barbara gave the names to the young man. She was proud that her sons held such prestigious positions.

The seas had settled enough for the porter to bring out the tray of drinks and Barbara helped herself to a large brandy. "I believe this will settle my nerves," she said. "I am glad that part of the voyage is behind us."

Two days later the steamer berthed in Napier and the passengers all disembarked. The ferry to Wellington would leave next day and in the meantime Barbara was driven to a hotel near the wharf where she would spend the night. It felt strange to be on firm land again after the motion of the ship and she was happy to relax in the comfort of the grand hotel for the night.

The coastal steamer to Wellington was smaller and quite crowded and this time Barbara shared a cabin with another woman. Thankfully it was only for two nights so it wasn't worth unpacking her bag.

She had to make do with sponging herself down while still in her underwear and looked forward to a hot bath when she arrived at her son's home. A liberal sprinkle of scented powder was the best she could do until then.

Chapter 6

Meanwhile in Wellington, Ellen was anticipating the arrival of her mother-in-law with mixed feelings. She had heard Francis speak of his mother and they had corresponded from time to time, but the two women had never met and Ellen was anxious to make a good impression.

Young Frank couldn't recall his grandmother but Clara had met her in Auckland while she was living with her grandparents. She remembered a pretty lady with dark hair piled up and a sweet smile coming to the farm to visit them. She knew she was a sister to Uncle Samuel who owned a property alongside her grandparents' farm.

 Little William was gaining weight and smiling at everyone, especially young Frank who still persisted in trying to hand him toys. "Your brother is too little to hold that bear. But he loves to hear you speak to him." Ellen encouraged the attention, knowing that Frank could feel resentful if he was ignored.

Clara was happiest when she was able to ride Whiskey and most days Maggie would escort her along the parade to the Jones' property. George had summoned up the courage to invite Maggie to a dance to be held at the tea gardens and she had agreed.

She asked Ellen's advice about what she should wear and Ellen was only to happy to help her. "It is so pleasant that my maid should seek my help. I do hope that this George is a decent young man who will respect her.'

"He seems like a fine lad and Maggie is happy to be with him. The Jones family speaks highly of him." Francis had noticed the blossoming friendship between the two young people and was eager to encourage it.

He was excited at the prospect of a visit from his mother, a cheerful character who made the best of every situation. "I know you and my mother will be great friends. She will be tired after her voyage but will be ready to look around our town as soon as she has recovered."

When the coastal ferry eventually tied up to the wharf in Wellington, Francis was standing on the jetty looking out for his mother. He waved when he saw her and she smiled and came towards him. The luggage was unloaded and piled onto the carriage and then they were headed along the waterfront towards Oriental Bay.

This was just Barbara's second visit to Wellington and she was amazed at the development since she had visited several years before following the sad death of Francis' first wife Maria whom she had known in Auckland.

In the last few years many of the buildings had become more substantial while the central town area was becoming over crowded with dozens of simple cottages crammed together. As they drove further around the bay, she marvelled at the gracious homes which were starting to appear on the lower slopes of Mt Victoria and along the parade.

When they turned into the entrance to the Stevens' home she gasped in surprise. "You have built a most elegant home, my dear. You must be very proud."

"It is mostly Ellen's doing. Without her I would still be living in that small cottage in the middle of town."

They turned the horse and carriage over to the groundsman and Francis carried the luggage inside. Frank had run down the steps to greet them and Ellen stood in the hallway with young Clara beside her.

"Welcome. I am so pleased you are here. We have been looking forward to this day for a very long time." Ellen held her arms out and greeted Barbara warmly. The hug was a little restrained but that was Ellen's way.

"Maggie will show you to your room and you might like to wash and tidy up after your long journey. I hate to think what conditions were like on the small steamer." Ellen bustled Barbara inside.

"The first steamer wasn't too bad but the small ferry was a different story. What I really need is a nice hot bath." Barbara followed Maggie up the stairs and into a large airy room decorated in the latest shades of rose and mauve. She selected some clean clothing from her luggage and let herself into the bathroom along the hallway where the tin bathtub had been filled and soft towels laid out.

"Thank you Maggie. This looks like heaven. I will have a long soak and then I will feel human again." Barbara closed the door and shed her clothing. She lowered herself into the bathtub and sighed. What a beautiful home. Francis was very fortunate to have such a grand place to raise his children.

A short time later Barbara was dressed and ready to face the family. They were all gathered in the living room which overlooked the bay. From the dormer windows a glorious vista could be enjoyed.

"This is so beautiful. But now I am anxious to get to know my grandchildren. Clara, you have grown into a beautiful child and this must be Frank. My, what a handsome lad." Barbara hugged the children then turned to Ellen. "You are so good to these children. Francis was truly blessed the day he met you."

"I have also been most fortunate. Francis is a good husband to me and we are very happy." Ellen smiled. She knew she would get on well with this pleasant woman. "But now you must meet your youngest grandson." Ellen led her mother-in-law into the nursery where William was just waking from his sleep. He lay quietly, looking around him.

There were tears in Barbara's eyes as she gazed at the precious baby. Francis had already lost a son and a daughter but she knew she was looking at a fine, healthy boy. "May I hold him?" she asked. "Certainly," Ellen replied and Barbara carefully picked up the baby and held him close. He gave her an uncertain smile and grabbed her finger with his fist.

"My, you are a strong little chap. Let me look at you. I swear you have your father's chin and look at all that dark hair. That must have come from you, Ellen." Barbara laughed as the baby screwed up his face and opened his mouth as though expecting to be fed. She handed him back to Ellen who carried him through to the small sitting room where she sat in the nursing chair.

"I will just give him his feed and then I will join you," she said. "In the meantime, Francis can show you the rest of the house."

The next few minutes passed happily as Francis pointed out all the features of his fine new home. The upper level comprised a number of living rooms and several bedrooms as well as two bathrooms and the nursery.

The curved staircase opened onto a grand entrance hall and Francis' office and a library with shelves of heavy, leather-bound books. Further back they came to a kitchen and formal dining room with the large oval table and high-backed chairs.

The servants' quarters were housed in a separate wing of the house and the back door led outside to the laundry room and garden. Barbara had already noted the stables and yards on her arrival.

"This really is a fine mansion. It must have cost a pretty penny. You are obviously doing very well my son."

"As I said before, most of it is due to Ellen who is already planning to build another house a short distance up the street. She will be able to lease it out for a good amount I am sure."

Barbara was astounded that Ellen should have such a good head for business. "Maybe we need to enlist her to work in your father's firm. He could sometimes do with a bit of good advice."

Francis laughed. He knew full well his father's strengths and failings. "How is he getting on with the latest project? A new type of paddle wheel to propel steamers I believe."

"Like most of his ideas, the beauty is in the creation. They seldom grow to maturity." Barbara smiled and looked across at Clara who had been walking behind them as they explored the house. "Maybe you would like to show me your room and then I could see where Frank sleeps.'

The children took Barbara's hand and they were soon climbing the stairs and heading for the nursery. Their toys and books were all arranged on shelving and a low table and chairs was set in the corner. "We play in here when the baby is awake. Otherwise we have to go somewhere else." Frank explained.

Clara was anxious to show off her beautiful room which Ellen had decorated with care. Exquisite beading hung from the walls and a lacy canopy covered a frame above the bed. "I pretend I am living in a tent. It is very cosy when the wind is loud." Clara was not really a ribbon and lace kind of girl but enjoyed having her own bedroom after living in a crowded farmhouse.

Frank was tugging at Barbara's hand, anxious to show off his own room which had been decorated with a nautical theme. Shelving, which ran along the side of the room, held every type of stuffed toy available as well as a collection of model boats of every shape and size.

"I can play in here when the baby is asleep in the nursery. It is just as much fun." Barbara smiled at the small child. What a bad start the little boy had had with his mother and brother both dying while he was still a baby. He had been placed in the care of a relative until Francis and Ellen were able to give him a home.

But now Ellen had finished feeding the baby and he lay on a rug kicking his legs in the air. "Do sit down and I will ask Maggie to bring us some tea. I hope the children haven't totally worn you out."

"No indeed. It has been a pleasure to view your lovely home and the children are very lucky to be living here." Barbara was grateful that the younger woman was proving to be such a good mother to Francis' children. It could well have turned out badly.

The next hour passed pleasantly as they chatted and admired little William, then Barbara rested in her room for a short time until dinner was announced.

The next few days were happy ones for Barbara as she got to know Ellen and the children, She was keen to meet up with her son Walter and his wife and it was arranged that they would dine together at Francis and Ellen's home later in the week.

In the meantime she enjoyed the ambiance of the Oriental Bay mansion and walked across the road each day to escort the children to the beach, where they splashed in the rock pools and swam when the tide was full.

When Francis was able to take time off work he drove his mother into the centre of town where she shopped and drank tea in the elegant dining rooms. Wellington was certainly every bit as grand as Auckland with its waterfront area and rows of business houses and stores rising up towards the hills.

Ellen was getting bored with the demands of her small child and ready to begin socialising. The dinner party to host Francis' brother and family would be a welcome change and she carefully planned the menu and supervised Maggie as she cleaned the best silver and ironed the fine Irish linen.

They had seen little of Walter and Emily since their little boy had been born but now the child was two years old. Barbara had only seen him once as a small baby when she had last come to Wellington.

"It seems that I have more grandchildren living in Wellington than I have back home. I only have Herbert's four young ones in Auckland and I'm not sure what sort of reception I will get if I visit as Jane's family has taken over her affairs."

"I'm sure Jane will always treat you kindly, mother. It wasn't your fault that her husband left her." Francis was sorry that his brother had left them in such an awkward situation. He knew that many would turn away from the family once the scandal had occurred.

On the evening of the dinner party, Ellen dressed carefully. She was already able to get back into most of her garments and wanted something elegant but not too ornate. She chose a gown in dark blue brocade with covered buttons down the front and a deep lace collar. The sapphire necklace that had belonged to her mother and silver ear rings would be perfect.

The children were to eat earlier in the kitchen and then spend some time with the adults before the main meal was served. Clara knew that she would be in charge as they played in the nursery until Maggie was free to put them to bed. Baby William would sleep in his mother's dressing room so he would not be disturbed.

If all went according to plan it would be a most civilized evening. But little Charles Stevens had other ideas. From the moment the guests arrived he clung to his mother's hand and refused to leave her side. "You really are being very naughty, Charles." Emily was embarrassed. She and Walter had kept their son at home with them since he was born and this was their first outing in a long time.

"I'm sorry our son is not used to dinner parties. He will have to remain with us or there will be a terrible tantrum," Walter said. Clara and Frank stared at the obstinate child in amazement. Surely he would like to share the toys in the nursery and enjoy the delicious tea which the cook had prepared.

Barbara tried not to interfere but could see that Ellen's careful plans were beginning to unravel. "Come on Charles. I will take you to the kitchen and see what cook has ready for you."

Charles grasped his mother's hand even tighter. "I will go with the children and help with their meal. You all stay and enjoy a drink and a chance to chat." Emily led little Charles from the room and followed the other children down the stairs to the kitchen where a few tasty treats had been laid out for them.

"My word, aren't we the lucky ones." Emily handed Charles a thinly sliced sandwich filled with ham and encouraged the other children to make their selections. Soon they were sitting happily around the table while Emily poured them a cool drink from a tall glass jug.

Soon Barbara joined them and there was happy laughter as the children made short work of the sandwiches and savouries. "I think it is time for dessert," said Barbara and she carried the sweet dishes from the serving bench and laid them on the table.

Delicate cakes with coloured topping, chocolate biscuits and plates of fruit were greeted with whoops of joy. Even little Charles picked up a cake in one hand and a luscious grape in the other.

By this time Ellen came down to see what was going on. She had stayed in the living room with the men for a time, but thought better of it when the women and children failed to appear. In spite of the fact that her careful plans had been spoiled, she had to smile when she took in the scene.

"It looks as though I am missing a great party. I am afraid that I am not experienced in these matters."

Barbara felt a little sorry for her daughter-in-law. "You are learning very fast my dear. It is to your credit that you have made a home for two grown children." She patted Ellen on the arm and urged her to sit and join them. The men would be happy in their own company until the meal was served.

Chapter 7

Barbara remained in Wellington for a month, then made the return journey, once again taking the two steamers. Her husband was waiting at the pier in Auckland to welcome her. It had been a long, lonely time without his wife and he had spent a great deal of time considering their future.

He waited until Barbara was settled back in their Grafton home before discussing Sydney's imminent departure to the South Island. "I have been thinking about closing the share broking business and concentrating on land sales. I feel that is where the future lies and as I am not getting any younger, the work will be less stressful."

Indeed, Barbara could see that Francis had aged in the short time she had been away. His hair was now mostly grey and his bristling beard a mixture of grey and black. "It sounds like a good move. We could probably sell some of our holdings and maybe it is time to move to a smaller home. This house is costly to run with all the rooms which we never use and such a large acreage."

Now that they were living alone, it seemed a waste to be paying the lease on the Grafton mansion and employing the number of staff it took to maintain it.

Francis had always enjoyed the prestige of living in the fine house, but his standing in the town had dropped since the scandal involving his son. He had enjoyed the heady days when Stevens and Sons Share brokers and Money lenders had been an important company. Now each of his sons had gone their own way and he had no desire to carry on alone.

Over the next few weeks he handed his clients over to a young man who was willing to pay a small amount to buy the business. Francis knew he would do well as he had recently arrived from London where he had worked for the Stock Exchange and had maintained strong contacts with the mother country.

"The business is changing with fewer mining rights being sold and more interest in real estate," he said as he looked around the office for the last time and shook the new owner by the hand. He was relieved that the amount he had received would help cover the expenses he had incurred.

He reluctantly relinquished the lease on the Grafton property and began looking around for a suitable replacement. A small weatherboard villa just off Queen Street took his eye. It was an ideal position for his real estate office and he would persuade Barbara to help with the administration.

The next week a new sign was placed in the window of the villa and Francis was back in business. He worded an advertisement for the newspaper advertising his properties at Takapuna which was across the harbour from the main town. There was a ferry service running over to Stokes Point where a few service shops had been built.

"I know that Takapuna will prove to be a popular place to live in the near future. It is just a short ride from the ferry and we currently own almost 150 acres there." The land was divided into several titles, including a small lot in the village and Francis was hoping that the sale of the properties would free up some capital which he desperately needed.

Barbara was more than willing to help out in the office. She could manage to care for the small house which had no garden but a field for Francis' horse. Answering a few queries would help fill in her day.

They would not miss the Takapuna land as the only time Francis visited his lots was to shoot the pheasants which roamed around freely in the thick bush which ran down to a long, sandy beach.

"I will take the boat to Stokes Point tomorrow, then ride over to the properties and check out the boundaries. Perhaps you could arrange to have some suitable notices made which can be placed on the land." Francis felt a surge of positive energy. They would soon be back in profit again.

Francis was able to walk the short distance from their house to the waterfront where he waited for the small craft that would ferry him the short distance to the nearest point of land on the other side. The North Auckland Hotel was flourishing and a general store and butchery were well established.

It was an easy matter to hire a horse from the livery stable and soon Francis was riding along the water's edge to where the wide sandy beach took over from the swampland.

His properties were spread over a wide area and it was a day's ride to get from one side of the peninsula to the other. Much of the land had been roughly cleared with fire leaving the slopes covered in barren scoria where native and introduced vegetation was struggling to survive.

The eastern side looked more promising with sunny hillsides overlooking the volcanic island of Rangitoto.

"This 80 acres should bring the best price. I will market it as a very desirable property," he said to himself as he banged the sturdy post into the ground with the painted sign 'For Sale. Apply F Stevens, Queen Street Auckland'.

Exhausted from his busy day, he returned the horse to the livery stable and called at the hotel for a drink before taking the boat back over the harbour. The publican soon struck up a conversation. He was keen to know why a businessman should be visiting this backwater. When he learned of the land for sale he showed an interest.

"I remember about 10 years ago that all the land at Alandale in the Parish of Takapuna was for sale. It was supposed to be the start of a whole new settlement."

"That is true. At the time I gave land for a church and school, but development has been slow and there has not been as much progress as some people would like. I think you have more chance of development here."

"We have the brick works and the candle factory and the ferry keeps me busy from time to time. I'm not complaining." The publican poured Francis a pint of ale and set about polishing the glasses.

As the ferry drew away from the northern shore, Francis looked back at the quiet village. His mind was always active. What if someone was to build a bridge from Auckland to Stokes Point? That would open up the whole area and his land would be worth a fortune.

Maybe he should come up with a plan and show it to the provincial council. But they were too busy investing in railways at present. Work had already begun on the route from Auckland to Onehunga, a town which rivalled

Auckland in growth as steamers were calling as they made their way through the treacherous seas of the west coast.

Francis sighed. There was so much potential all around him. If only he had access to unlimited finance he could change the world.

Barbara had been busy in his absence with many enquiries for rental properties as well as houses to buy. They urgently needed new listings and she wrote out an advertisement for the newspaper and took it into the office. The clerk recognized her and asked how business was going.

"We have only just begun concentrating on property sales, but indications are positive," she said. She picked up a few provisions at the general store and carried them home in a basket. She was enjoying being back in charge of her own kitchen, something she hadn't done for a number of years.

By the time Francis arrived back at the house she had prepared a simple meal of beef and boiled vegetables, followed by apple pie with cream. They settled down for a drink while Francis filled her in on the day's events.

"I can see the time when the northern shore will be the most sought after place to live. Can you imagine a great bridge spanning the gap to Stokes Point?"

Barbara smiled. She was used to Francis and his wild plans. She well knew that by tomorrow he would be thinking of some other scheme.

"We will need to get more properties to sell. I have been busy with enquiries today but we have very few listings. Most people want a modest house to buy or something to rent."

"We will drop leaflets around the town and let people know we are in business. But I have some other ideas I want to work on."

As soon as the meal was finished Francis got out his drawing book and pencil. He was soon sketching a rough outline of an arched bridge with two lanes for horse-drawn carriages. There were tall pillars at intervals to take the weight and he was busy estimating the amount of steel needed for such a project.

Large quantities of steel were being shipped over from England to build the railways. Perhaps some of this could be diverted to a harbour crossing. He worked away happily until it was too dark to see. Barbara sighed. She would need to keep Francis' mind on track if the real estate business was to succeed.

Next day was Sunday and the office was closed. Francis wasted no time in bringing out his plans for a harbour crossing and continued to sketch and calculate.

He had heard nothing back about his idea for an amphibious locomotive for transporting troops over land and water, even though the suggestion had been noted in the files of the Horse Guards in London. Neither did the British war office get back to him about an impregnable, invisible rotary battery for the protection of Her Majesty's ports and strategic passes in India.

And the thwarted plans for a railway line from Nelson still riled him. He had been all set to visit his wife's brother in London to seek the necessary funding. The province only had to grant him a substantial acreage in payment. It would have been cheap land taken from the Maori people and he would have had no qualms about accepting it.

Barbara was disappointed that he was not sharing the time with her. It would have been the perfect chance to walk around the town dropping off leaflets advertising their business and seeking properties to sell and rent.

"Come on, my dear. I really want your company this afternoon. We could walk to the old Albert Park Barracks and see whether any progress has been made. I read that the Auckland Improvement Commission is organizing a landscape design competition now that the barracks have been closed."

The Albert Barracks had been constructed in 1847 and was the largest British military fortification in the country. The Colonial Government had recently abandoned the project and now 15 acres of land had been set aside as a ground for recreation and amusement. It was hoped that a public garden would be created with space for monuments and statues to commemorate famous people.

Francis put down his pencil. "That could be interesting. They say there are some prestigious houses being built in the area. We may be able to add some of these to our books."

They were soon dressed for the outdoors in long coats and hats and Francis carried a wooden cane with a bone handle. It was just a short walk along Queen Street to the old barracks which looked desolate and forlorn with broken buildings and piles of brick lying around.

"It would need someone with imagination to come up with a plan for this untidy area. The commission certainly has its work cut out to turn this into a beauty spot." Barbara looked around in dismay.

"I don't know. The land has some good features and once the rubble has been cleared there would be space for a glorious array of planting." Francis could visualise leafy English trees and flowering shrubs with low hedge borders and curving pathways. "There are enough bricks lying around to make steps and low walls. I think it would be a very exciting project to be involved in."

They walked around the surrounding area where the new houses were being built and placed leaflets through mail slots wherever possible. "I'm sure these villas will attract some very wealthy merchants. There are many suitable building sites available and the commission would do well to begin auctioning them off." Francis could see the possibilities in this raw environment.

"It is a shame you are not on the improvement commission. You would have everything sorted in no time." Barbara smiled at Francis' enthusiasm.

They wandered slowly back to their small dwelling, past the merchants' stores and simple cottages with picket fences. People were lounging on their porches while the children played in the streets.

It was very different from life out on the fringe of town at Grafton but there was a vibrancy about this young town that bode well for the future.

Chapter 8

Work was well underway on the new house in Oriental Bay. The site was set back from the street and elevated with views over the harbour and distant hills. Ellen stopped to catch her breath as she climbed the steep incline and looked around her. There was space for three more houses between the new dwelling and their home on the corner of the parade.

"I want each house to have a view of the harbour so we must make sure that they are spaced accordingly," she said, as she consulted the architect who had drawn up the plans. "I wish to attract high class tenants who will be willing to pay a substantial rent."

"You are very wise, Mrs Stevens. To build all the houses in a straight line would be a mistake. I'm sure you will have no problem securing good tenants when the time comes."

Ellen had enjoyed her mother-in-law's visit but now she would have more time to pursue her business interests. She was no longer breast feeding little William so he could be left with Maggie or the new maid who had been employed to give Maggie more time with the children.

An advertisement in the newspaper: 'Wanted, a clean, tidy girl for general housework. Must have references' had attracted eight young women who had all been nervous during their interview with the formidable Mrs Stevens.

Esther Jones had given birth to a little girl and Ellen had already paid her a visit and admired the new child. She was anxious, however, to meet more of the bay's residents but was not sure how to go about it.

Francis provided the solution when he announced that the son of the owner of the tea gardens was to marry and that he and Ellen had been invited to the reception. "Mr Wilkinson has invited all the homeowners along the parade to share afternoon tea next Saturday, following the wedding. It will be a great chance to meet the other residents." Francis handed Ellen the invitation.

"What an excellent idea. I will be able to wear the new gown I ordered before my pregnancy and I'm sure I have a suitable hat that no-one has seen before." Ellen was thrilled that at last there was to be a social event they could attend without the children. She would talk to as many people as she could and decide who to invite to their home in the hear future.

Francis smiled. His wife was content as long as there was something going on. He was still a little nervous about the plans to build houses on the Hay Street allotments, because even though Ellen had access to funds, a small mortgage would be necessary to complete the first of the residences. This would be paid from the rental received as long as they could attract a secure tenant.

His job as clerk in the Crown Lands department paid a steady income which covered the upkeep of their home but Ellen had extravagant tastes when it came to clothing and furniture.

She had received many fine pieces of china and silverware from her parents over the years had begun to collect works of art which adorned the walls of their home. Her latest acquisition had been oil paintings of Mount Earnshaw and Lake Taupo which took pride of place in the entrance hall.

The children interrupted his thoughts at this time. He could hear them playing happily in the nursery and popped his head in the door to speak with them. "Hi Poppa." Frank was the first to notice him. "Come and play with us."

Francis was soon involved in building a play tent from sheets which were thrown over high-backed chairs. Clara had set up some cushions for seats but Francis couldn't quite let himself crawl under the sheet to join the children. "I doubt that I would be able to get back on my feet," he laughed as Frank tried to persuade him to join them in the tent.

He was pleased to escape to the comfort of the small sitting room where Ellen was sitting in an upholstered chair with little William perched on her knee. "Look how bonny our little boy is. He likes to smile at me."

Francis went across to his small son. He was certainly growing fast and he held out his arms for his father to take him. He felt awkward but held the child stiffly in his arms and carried him across the room to the large bay window.

"See, my boy. You will be able to play on that beach any time soon. "

Ellen smiled at the sight of her husband holding their child. He had missed out on so much with his other two children as, until now, they had lived with their dead mothers' families. She was sure he would get close to William and learn to love him as she did.

Wilkinson's Tea Gardens had been gaily decorated for the big event. David Wilkinson's son, also named David, and his new bride Annie had been married earlier in the day at St Peters Church, Te Aro, and arrived by horse-drawn carriage as the guests assembled.

The tea rooms had been set up with white linen table cloths and red bows while the silverware and glasses sparkled in the sunlight that streamed through the windows. Ellen and Francis had been seated with Captain and Mrs Jones as well as half a dozen strangers who were soon introducing each other.

Francis was particularly drawn to a young engineer, William Hale, who worked for the government in the Public Works Department. It turned out that William was married to the daughter of Mr Wilkinson, and lived on a property close to the tea gardens.

Francis struck up a conversation with the young man and learned that he was currently supervising the building of a lighthouse on Farewell Spit at the very top of the South Island. "This project must take you away from home a great deal. I'm sure Farewell Spit must be one of the most remote places on earth."

"It surely is, but I spend much of my time back here in the office in Wellington. I visit the site each week. It is quite an adventure getting there and I usually stay two nights." William was a most affable fellow and introduced his wife to Ellen.

"I am planning a dinner party next week. Would you and your husband like to join us?" Ellen liked the look of the young woman who had lived all her life at Oriental Bay. She wanted to make the most of the opportunity and decided to extend the invitation to all the guests at their table. Eight people would make for a very congenial evening.

A delicious meal was laid out and served by immaculate waitresses. All manner of fresh and roast vegetables were on offer as well as generous slices of meat and poultry. A range of sauces was also available.

As the guests enjoyed their meal, a string quartet played in the background. Ellen, resplendent in her elaborate gown and finest jewellery, was most content. This was the life she had been dreaming about.

Next day was Sunday and Francis decided it was time the family attended a church service. It was some time since they had been to the church where he had twice been married and he thought it was high time that young Clara was introduced to the local parish.

"Do I have to? Maggie was going to take me riding on her day off." Clara pouted. She had regularly attended church back in her country village and had found it quite a dull experience.

"There will be plenty of time for riding when we return. Your father is right. We will all go, except for little William who can stay back with Maggie." Ellen liked the idea of riding in their carriage through the town to the church which they had regularly attended when they were living in Ghuznee Street.

"We will show you where your father was living when we first met. That was before we built this house and moved out here to the bay." Ellen directed the children to their rooms where they dressed into tidy clothes and were soon ready for the trip into town.

Frank was once again excited at the sight of the ships anchored in the bay and the small coastal steamers and fishing boats tied to the piers. "Our beach hasn't any boats like this. I wish they would anchor near our house."

Francis spoke sternly. "We do not want a boat launch in our beautiful bay. It is the only beach close to town that can be enjoyed by everyone." He was afraid that someone would want to spoil the bay by building boat sheds and piers in front of their property.

They turned away from the waterfront and up the hill towards the small wooden church. A row of carriages and carts had already assembled with the horses being tethered to rails and given a nose bag filled with grain.

The Rev Stock was standing on the front steps to welcome his parishioners and his face lit up when he saw Francis and Ellen with the two children in tow. "I am pleased to see you all looking so well and these are your dear children. Welcome to St Peter's."

"We also have a baby son at home." Ellen was all smiles as she greeted the minister. "We will make arrangements soon for him to be baptized."

The family went inside and found an empty pew. Francis and Ellen knelt down for a few minutes and gave a prayer of thanks for their good fortune while the children stared at the wooden pulpit and the stained glass windows and tried not to wriggle about.

An hour later, after listening to a dreary sermon and joining in the well-known hymns, they shared a warm drink and biscuits and climbed onto the carriage for the journey home. Luckily the sun was shining though a strong wind blew and it wasn't long before the horse was led into the yard and the family sat down to a light lunch which had been prepared in their absence.

Maggie was impatient to take Clara for her promised pony ride. She hadn't seen George since the dance the week before and she was eager to speak with him again.

Although it was his day off, he was waiting near the barn when they arrived and helped Clara saddle the little pony. "Up you go, young Clara. You should be able to manage on your own today. I think you are ready to take the track up the hill. It will bring you back along Hay Street past your father's house."

Clara felt very important as she encouraged Whiskey to trot up the hill along the narrow track which wound its way through long grass and stunted bushes. Halfway up the hill the track veered to the left and soon joined up with the stony road leading down to the bay.

She kept the pony down to a walk as the grade was steep and soon she passed the building site where Ellen's new dwelling was being erected. It would have a grand view, even better than their own outlook, she decided.

She turned into her gateway in the hopes that her father would see her and laughed at the look of surprise on his face as he caught sight of her astride the small pony.

"Look Poppa. George said I could ride Whiskey up the track today. He is behaving very well."

"Goodness my dear. That is very brave of you. Now take care along the parade as there could be other riders or carriages about today."

Clara rode carefully back to the Jones' property and was just in time to see Maggie jump guiltily away from George's arms as they enjoyed a precious time together.

George blushed bright red and came quickly over to take the pony's reins as Clara jumped down from the saddle. "I would like to unsaddle Whiskey myself and make him comfortable. We are in no hurry to return home," she said, giving Maggie a warm smile.

Maggie sat down beside George and they watched as Clara skillfully tended to the pony and let him go in the yard. "I so enjoyed the dance. Would you like to go again?"

George had been trying to summon the courage to ask the question and gave a sigh of relief when Maggie agreed to accompany him again. She would not be free that week, however, as Ellen had arranged a dinner party and needed Maggie to supervise the children.

"It will have to be next week, but I will come here whenever I have some free time and we could walk on the beach," she said.

"That would be grand. My employers would let me have time to myself if there is nothing urgent to attend to." George could hardly believe his luck that this lovely girl would want to walk with him. "I will see you again soon then."

Maggie was smiling to herself as they walked the short distance back to the Stevens' home. Clara glanced in her direction once in a while, not too sure what to make of it, but as long as Maggie wanted to see George, there would be plenty of chances to ride the pony.

Chapter 9

After their walk to the old Albert Park barracks, Francis put aside his plans for a harbour crossing and began drawing out sketches of a park with walkways, walls and ornate statues. Barbara smiled as she called him for tea.

Her husband was never happy unless he was designing some project or other. It would be good if he ever followed up his ideas. There were several patents in his name and the most likely had been a machine for splitting shingles which he had invented soon after arriving in New Zealand. Shingle roofs were popular and the idea had great potential, but the necessary finance had not been forthcoming and the patent languished in an office drawer.

Over the meal they discussed their plans for the next day. Francis had a number of enquiries to follow up and Barbara would keep the office open. She was looking forward to the challenge but was weary after their long walk and fell asleep early.

Next morning Francis set off early on foot to deliver advertising fliers around the business houses in Queen Street and along the harbour's edge. There must be plenty of people needing new homes or accommodation and they urgently needed new listings before they could satisfy their clients.

Since the scandalous affair involving their son, Francis had noticed that many of his acquaintances were no longer friendly. Several had been left out of pocket by Herbert's sudden disappearance and although they knew that Francis was not responsible for his son's debts, they were wary of doing business with him.

Barbara's morning started off slowly with two men enquiring about rental properties. They looked rather poor and downtrodden and she doubted that they could afford the rents for the few listings they had available.

The next visitor, however, was well dressed and very annoyed. "Mrs Stevens, I have been victimized by your son to the extent of over 200 pounds. What are you going to do about it?"

Barbara was taken aback. "I'm sorry about that, sir, but there is not much I can do for you. Our son's business transactions were totally separate from that of my husband."

"Even so. Surely your conscience is getting the better of you and you would be prepared to settle some of your son's debts. I know your husband still owns a considerable amount of property which could be sold."

"That would be between my husband's lawyer and your own to sort out, so if you don't mind, sir, I have other work to attend to." Barbara was shaking inwardly, but tried to appear calm on the outside as she showed the irate gentleman to the door and ushered him out.

Once he was outside on the pavement, she sunk into a chair and put her head in her hands. "Damn you, Herbert," she muttered to herself. "I hope you are not going to leave us with a big mess to clean up."

Francis returned a short time later and when he heard of the visit he was very concerned. "My dear wife, I hope you are not going to have to face any more callers like that. Let's hope that it was not typical of what people are saying about us. If that is the case, then I fear our real estate business is doomed."

"What can we do, Francis? I don't really want to remain in Auckland if there is a shadow hanging over us. We are no longer young and I would like us to live out our days in peace." Barbara hated the thought of facing any more conflict. There had been a time when they lived in London and their business was in trouble. On the recommendation of her brother Samuel Vickers they had made the big move to New Zealand to start a new life. She did not want to go through times like that again.

They sat in the living room of their small rented house, fearful of what lay ahead. It looked as though the successful days were over and some major changes would need to be made.

With so much on her mind, Barbara sat down to draft a letter to her son Francis. He had a good head on his shoulders and should be able to offer them some sound advice. Perhaps it was time to try their luck in a different town where no-one knew of the scandal that was affecting their family name.

She thought about the good years and the bad that she had shared with her husband. At first they ran a school in their home in Chigwell where a number of pupils boarded while receiving tuition.

When Francis gave up teaching and joined a stock broking firm, they moved to Strawbroy Lodge in Surrey where they employed a governess for their children as well as three female servants and a gardener. Young Francis joined his father in the stock broker's practice for a short time before he left for New Zealand about a year before the rest of the family.

Barbara sighed when she recalled the grand manner in which they had lived on the outskirts of London. Servants and carriages and all the beautiful clothes she could wear. But she had loved her husband through good times and bad and knew that they would survive another disaster.

A week went by before Francis received his mother's letter. He picked up the mail from the brass tray beside the front door and took it into his office. Most of the letters contained bills to be paid and there were two invitations for Ellen to reply to. He sat down in an armchair and poured a small brandy before he opened the letter from Barbara.

"This is not good news," he said to Ellen, who had just come into the room carrying little William. "My parents are facing hard times and I'm not sure what we can do to help them."

Francis read out the contents of the letter and was dismayed that his father had closed the business and moved out of the fine house at Grafton. "They are renting a small cottage right in the centre of town and trying to run a real estate office from the premises."

He read on, full of concern that his parents, who had worked hard and raised a large family, should be living in such humble conditions.

"Your brother Herbert has a lot to answer for. Who knows how many creditors will come knocking on your parents' door?" Ellen shared her husband's concerns. "It might be best if they moved to a different part of the country. After all, apart from Jane and the children, there is no family left in Auckland."

"You could be right my dear. They would be better off in Wellington where Walter and I could keep an eye on them."

Ellen nodded. "It would be delightful to have your mother living close by. I found her to be a most pleasant lady."

"That is so, but my father can be a bit of a trial at times. He is always coming up with some scheme or other but does not manage his finances too well." Francis was pleased that he had never been associated with his father's business. Working for the government was a much safer option, although the rewards were not very great.

Francis decided to write to his parents and propose that they move to Wellington. He knew that Barbara would be delighted to see more of her grandchildren and she would be good company for Ellen.

Saturday night was a time for entertainment in the growing town of Wellington. Ellen was determined that her dinner party would be a night to remember and one that would launch her on the social scene.

She had selected the menu with care and was satisfied that the cook would carry out her instructions. The new servant girl, Annie, would be serving the food while Maggie was responsible for looking after the children.

The main living room was charmingly decorated with bowls of flowers and bright silk cushions on the long couches. Ellen knew that her guests would wish to admire the view from the large bay windows, so the curtains had been drawn back and tied with silken cord.

Captain James Jones and his wife Esther were the first to arrive. Esther was pleased to be having an evening away from the children and beamed as she looked around the attractive room. "It is such a treat to be out with my husband without the children trying to claim my attention."

She sat down in a comfortable armchair and accepted a glass of brandy from young Annie.

"I totally agree with you. The children will be allowed to meet our guests and then Maggie will keep them entertained. She is very good with the children." Ellen settled on the long sofa, holding a slender glass of white wine.

"I know our young lad, George, is very fond of your Maggie. It would be most pleasant if they made a match of it." Esther had a romantic streak in her nature.

Their conversation was interrupted as the other guests all arrived at the same time and there was a flurry of activity as coats were hung up and everyone was seated. Trays of drinks as well as plates of delicious canapés were set up on a side table and Francis took over the role of host.

The buzz of conversation grew more animated as the drinks were enjoyed and when Maggie brought the children to the door the women crowded around little William admiring him while Clara and Frank stood awkwardly in the middle of the room, looking around them.

Esther Jones was soon chatting with Clara as she was getting to know her well and Maria Hale took pity on Frank and beckoned him to sit beside her. Ellen did not want the children to stay too long and soon indicated to Maggie that is was time for them to withdraw.

"What sweet children." The adults settled down with their drinks until Annie informed them that dinner was ready. Ellen led the way as the guests descended the stairs, taking in the fine paintings and tapestries that hung on the walls.

The dining room was on the lower floor adjacent to the kitchen and once everyone was seated, they were served with bowls of soup and crusty bread. Ellen had taken the opportunity to use the Royal Doulton dinner service which her family had brought out from Ireland.

She looked around proudly as her guests relaxed and enjoyed the delicious food on offer. Pheasant and tender lamb with roasted vegetables and tender green beans with homemade sauces and the finest English mustard met with approval.

"You must congratulate your cook, Ellen. She has done a magnificent job." Esther Jones was first to compliment her.

By the time the chocolate dessert was consumed, accompanied by a glass of sweet sherry, everyone was ready to retire to the living room where a variety of teas was available.

It was some time before the last of the guests departed and Ellen was tired but too excited to sleep. "That was a very successful evening. I am sure we will receive many invitations in the near future."

"I do hope so, dear Ellen. You were a charming host and I know everyone thoroughly enjoyed their meal. But now it is time for bed." Francis was exhausted but proud of his wife's efforts. He was sure she would receive many thank you notes and hopefully, a few invitations.

Chapter 10

Francis Worrell Stevens was not having a good week. The only bright spot had been an offer to buy a portion of his land at Takapuna, although the price offered was below expectations.

"What am I to do, Barbara? That is the finest piece of land on the northern shore but we really need the money so I suppose we will have to accept it." Francis shuffled the papers on his desk. He had drawn up the plans for the subdivision with the streets named after his sons, grandson and brother in law. Even Herbert's name was included although Francis had toyed with the idea of excluding him.

Barbara was becoming increasingly nervous as she faced the few people who came in the door. They were either unsuitable as tenants or gentlemen asking for repayment of their losses. Thankfully most were polite and several apologized for causing any embarrassment, but as they pointed out, the money was owed to them and they wanted payment.

"They think that we are responsible for Herbert's debts as he was part of your company for so long. I can't see this problem going away in a hurry."

"I'm afraid that Herbert was guilty of tracing his clients' signatures onto sales agreements and then pocketing the proceeds. He must have got away with a tidy sum." Francis had been investigating his son's activities. He would probably be close to America by now with his young bride.

"Do you think Miss Paul knew that Herbert was already married? If so, she is as guilty as he is. She must have been beguiled by our son's charms to be part of such a deception." Barbara was amazed that a young woman would be prepared to go to such lengths to be with a man.

"The family claims she is innocent, but they obviously don't want their good name tarnished. It seems that we are the ones who are being punished."

Francis decided that it was high time he visited Jane Stevens and the children who had been left by their father. He decided to make the short journey to Parnell the next day and set off early on his favourite gelding.

He had not seen Jane since her husband's departure although he had tried to make contact a number of times. Hopefully she would not be blaming him for what Herbert had done. The house looked deserted when he rode into the driveway. The curtains were pulled and the blinds drawn. He dismounted and knocked on the solid front door, but was met with silence. She and the children must have gone away to avoid the creditors who were no doubt giving her a hard time.

Francis thought that they were probably staying with her brothers at Waipuna, which was some distance away in the country. He would have to try and reach her another time. He was about to ride away when he heard the sound of horse's hooves on the gravel road. A mail contractor turned into the driveway and placed a bundle of letters though the slot in the door.

"I doubt that anyone is here right now. I fear that my daughter-in-law has abandoned the house."

"My job is to deliver the mail. What happens to the letters is not my concern." The mail man continued on to the next property, leaving Francis wondering what that pile of letters contained.

When Francis returned to their small cottage, Barbara was anxious to hear how Jane and the children were faring. "Unfortunately, the house was deserted. There is probably a large amount of mail that needs attending to and I'm not sure where Jane would have gone."

"My precious grandchildren! The youngest is just a baby. When will I see them again?" Barbara had been close to the children and would miss them dearly if they were kept away from her. "I think we should ride out to Waipuna as soon as possible and discuss the problem with Jane's family. I don't want her to think that we have abandoned them."

"You are right, my dear. We have been so involved with our own problems we have scarcely had time to consider poor Jane. With both her parents dead and four little ones she will need all the help she can get."

Barbara was inconsolable. "Remember their beautiful wedding at Panmure? They were such a perfect couple. But with four children born within six years, perhaps their relationship was becoming a little strained. Our son always had an eye for the ladies."

"That's all very well. Many a gentleman has sought his pleasure elsewhere, but absconding with a mere child, and taking his clients' money with him is unforgivable." It was unusual for Francis to show anger but his patience was running out.

Barbara couldn't stand the tension any longer and walked out of the room. She stood on the porch of the small cottage and looked out onto the busy street. How she wished she could be back at their comfortable home in Grafton with the trees and peaceful fields around her.

But it was no good feeling sorry for her self. She had learned that lesson many times over the years. Hopefully there would be a letter from one of their sons in the next few days which would help them decide their future.

The next day was warm and sunny so Francis was able to hire a dog cart to take them on the journey to Waipuna where Jane's family owned a large area of land. Although the acreage had been divided among the family on the death of their father, the two eldest brothers carried out the bulk of the farming.

There were several houses on the properties and it could take some time to track Jane and the children down so Barbara packed a loaf of bread and some hard boiled eggs as well as a container of ginger beer in case they were not home until late evening.

Before they knew it they were leaving the town behind them as they travelled along the sea's edge, then up and over the hill towards the town of Panmure where Herbert and Jane had been married in the small church of St Matthews.

As they skirted the ancient volcano, they could see the remnants of the fortifications built during the land wars. Many British soldiers had been camped in the area during those turbulent years and some had remained to take up the allotments granted to them.

Farms were beginning to flourish, with cattle and sheep grazing on the green pastures and clusters of houses here and there.

It took over an hour to reach their destination where Francis reigned in the tired horse and tethered him to a rail.

The land was close to an early mission station and Francis was soon asking questions about Jane and the children.

They were directed to the home of one of the brothers and it didn't take long to reach the largest of the houses on the main farm. Barbara was nervous about what sort of reception they would get but her desire to see their grandchildren over-rode her fears.

"I'm sure the children are close by. Jane's family is sure to be protecting them," she said, as they jolted along the stony driveway.

"I do hope so, Jane is lucky to have such a large family. They have always looked after each other." Francis sounded more confident than he felt as the large gabled homestead came into view.

As they approached, two large dogs rushed out, frightening the horse, but in spite of the noise, their tails were wagging and Francis knew they were friendly animals. A tall man was working in the yard beside the door and when he turned around, they realized that it was Jane's oldest brother James.

He came towards them and helped Barbara down from the carriage. "This is a surprise. I hope you have been keeping well." Francis was pleased that he did not appear to harbour any resentment towards them.

"We have been most anxious about Jane's welfare. This terrible time is affecting all of us." Francis followed James along the path that led to the front door.

"Are the children here with you? I have missed them so much and would love to see them." Barbara trailed behind them.

"I'm afraid they are not here but have gone to stay with Jane's sister Sophia and her husband at Hobson's Bay. You have come a long way for nothing." James led them into the house and through to a sunny living room which opened onto a wooden verandah.

"You must have some refreshments before you leave and tell me all you know of your son's departure." James was anxious to hear the whole story as there had been so much gossip spread around the town. He was a fair man and ready to listen to their point of view.

The next hour went by quickly as the men shared their knowledge of Herbert's actions. Barbara sat on a comfortable chair and dozed for a time. She was disappointed that she had missed the children but knew they would be in good hands with Sophia and her large family.

The journey home was uneventful and Francis felt more at ease after talking to Jane's brother. "At least our real friends are still accepting us. In a few weeks everything will return to normal."

Chapter 11

After the success of her dinner party, Ellen was overwhelmed with invitations to meet the other residents of the bay. A number of fine Victorian houses now graced the area and Francis was anxious that the beach front would remain open to all residents.

A rough track had been formed which led to the boat slip at Evans Bay, but this had created a belt of swamp in front of their properties. "Council is complaining about the use of public land, but I can understand why people are draining the swamp and planting flower gardens to beautify it. I will write to the councillors and persuade them to allow the gardens to be kept until the road is widened and a footpath formed."

In his position with the government, Francis' letters were usually well received. The council stopped complaining, the gardens flourished and the bay continued to attract many town dwellers.

But a short time later, an even bigger problem occurred. It was at a convivial dinner party held by Captain Jones, that Francis first heard the news. Two of their neighbours, Messrs Coffey and Dixon were proposing to build a slip to launch large ships right in front of their Hay Street properties.

Ellen was perturbed at the news but Francis was horrified. "Over my dead body," he declared in front of the polite gathering. "This beautiful bay and walkway will be preserved for ever. The ship yard must be built back towards the town."

They left the gathering earlier than Ellen would have liked, but there was no peace for Francis. "We must do everything we can to retain this beautiful stretch of harbour. I realise it is merely a rocky and often muddy place right now but with the addition of loads of sand and a building where swimmers can undress, it could be a beauty spot forever."

Ellen agreed. She didn't want an ugly ship building right across the road from their home. They would need to do something about it.

"We will start a petition and collect many hundreds of signatures," she vowed. "Tomorrow morning we will set up a table in front of our house and urge passersby to sign it."

"I agree," said Francis. "I will send people into the town on horseback to collect more signatures. This beautiful place will be a national treasure for ever."

It wasn't long before most of the residents living along the waterfront had signed the petition. "A boat slip would devalue our properties and close the only worthwhile walkway for the citizens of Wellington," they claimed.

A week later 250 people had signed the petition and many more would have signed. With such a level of protest, Coffey and Dixon decided to move their planned slipway further around the bay and the beach was left unscathed.

"You have done so well, my dear." Ellen was full of praise for her husband. She had just discovered that she was with child again and was happy to be giving young William a sibling. She hoped it would be the last, however, as she was now in her late 30s and although they were in a strong financial position she wanted to give their children a good start in life.

The first dwelling in Hay Street had been completed and Ellen was pleased to have leased it to a wealthy merchant who paid good money for such a prestigious address. Plans had already been drawn up for another house next door. This would have even more rooms and could be run as a boarding house, Ellen decided.

Francis was still worried about his parents and was eagerly awaiting a reply to his letter.
He didn't know what had become of Herbert's wife and children but knew they were the only family members left in Auckland. They had received good news from his brother Sydney who was enjoying his role in the postal service at Timaru. He hinted that he had met a delightful woman from Tasmania who had captured his heart.

"It seems as if our Sydney has fallen in love. He speaks highly of this Annie, who sounds like a very fine lady."

"I am so happy for Sydney. He is an honest and caring man. Your father should be proud of his sons."

"I'm sure that, apart from one, we have not let him down. We all have reputable careers with the government and admirable wives to sustain us." Francis was pleased that they were to have another child. Little William was growing up fast and Frank and Clara had settled well in their new home. Yes, life was very good indeed.

When Clara heard there was to be a new baby, she wasn't so sure. William was now toddling about and upsetting their games, and a new baby would claim much of Ellen's attention. But worse still, it would take up a lot of the servant girl Maggie's time. Would she still be able to accompany Clara to the Jones' household to ride little Whiskey?

By now she was so accomplished at riding the small pony that her father decided she could walk along the short stretch of road and bridle and saddle Whiskey with no help from Maggie or George.

Esther Jones agreed. As long as Clara stayed on the property she could come and go as she pleased. This arrangement did not, however, find favour with Maggie or George.   They had relied on Clara's riding lessons to give them time together. With another infant to care for, who knew when Maggie would ever be free to meet George, apart from her precious day off each week?

They had become accustomed to enjoying the dances at the tea gardens as long as Ellen didn't have a social engagement. Her activities had slowed down over recent weeks as she suffered from bouts of sickness, but Maggie knew her employer would be feeling well soon and ready to socialize more frequently.

"I love you so much George. I want to be with you forever," she sighed one night when they were finally alone.

"That makes me very happy, my love. Why then don't we get married and be together all the time?"

"Are you sure we would manage? Where would we live?" Maggie was caught by surprise. She would dearly love to be wed, but could they afford it? George took her in his arms, his firm body pressing against her.

"I have already spoken to my bosses and they have no objection to employing a married man. In fact, they said they would be delighted to have you in their household."

Their embrace was long and passionate, but Maggie broke away with a sigh. "There'll be plenty of time for that later, George my love. Let's walk on the beach now and talk about our future."

Clara was now approaching her 10th birthday and although Ellen was feeling the effects of her pregnancy she wanted to give the child a birthday to remember.

"I have decided to host a fancy dress party for the children. We will encourage them to dress in all sorts of costumes and entertainment will be arranged."

"Are you sure it won't be too much for you." Francis was worried about his wife as she seemed to tire easily. He still had sad memories of losing two wives through illness.

"I'm fine. I won't have to do much myself. We will hire a magician and our children's costumes can be created by my dressmaker. Maggie will supervise the young ones and Cook and Annie will serve the food."

Francis smiled at his wife's organizing skills. Once she made up her mind about something, it usually happened. It looked as though Clara was to have a great party.

Ellen set a date for two weeks' time and began to make a list of people to invite. Esther Jones and her brood would be top of the list and of course, Walter and Emily with little Charles.

"I don't actually know very many families with children. I suppose we will have to risk asking some of Clara's classmates although we won't know what type of children they might be." Ellen set down her pen with a frown on her face.

"I know that Clara will have her own ideas about that. I'm sure the girls who attend her school will be most suitable." Francis couldn't really see what the fuss was about. One child was much like another in his experience.

Clara came into the room at that moment and when she heard the news about a party her face lit up. "That would be such fun. I want all the girls in my class to come. Please let me invite them." She danced around the room in excitement.

"I suppose that would be alright, but are you sure they are well behaved? The house is not suitable for any unruly children." Ellen shuddered at the thought of what might happen to her precious furnishings and ornaments if a crowd of school girls was let loose."

Once Clara left the room Francis was able to tell Ellen what he had planned as her surprise birthday present. "I've seen how well Clara handles that little pony she rides, but now I think it is time she had one of her own. I have arranged for a fine pony to be delivered in time for the party."

"Oh Francis, she would be so happy to have her own mount but have we enough room to keep another animal?" Ellen was conscious of the fact that their property was scarcely large enough to accommodate their own horse.

"There is plenty of land on your allotments. We might have to upgrade the fencing but I'm sure there is space for one small animal." Francis knew that his daughter would be overwhelmed to have her own pony. She had ridden back on the farm south of Auckland and would be able to accompany him on rides around the town.

"I will ask Clara to write the names of her classmates and make out the invitations. She can take them to school on Monday. That will give them time to come up with a costume." Ellen was pleased to have something to organize, even if it was only a party for Clara.

There was much deliberation over the next few days before Frank chose to be an English soldier and Clara, a

Maori maiden, much to Ellen's surprise. She had forgotten that Clara had mixed with many Maori children while living up north and owned a precious piu piu or Maori skirt made from dried flax with an intricate woven pattern on the waistband.

"I will make my own head band. I just need some black and red paint to make the design," she decided.

Francis smiled. There was a lot to learn about his daughter. He knew he could find some of his old military gear to help out with Frank's costume, although a full-sized sword was probably out of the question.

With all the arrangements in place, Clara could hardly wait for the day of her party. At times she missed her grandparents back on the farm and wished she could see them, but Auckland was many miles from Wellington and the journey long and tedious.

Her costume was almost ready. All she needed was a plain black garment to wear under the piu piu. The headband had been made from stiff paper and decorated with a traditional Maori pattern and much to Ellen's disgust she would need no shoes.

There were 10 girls in her class at school and all but two were able to come to the party. Ellen had decided that the whole event would be held in the downstairs living area and dining room. The best of the ornaments had been moved but the rooms would still be bright with flowers, red and white camellias in the living area and spring bulbs in the dining room.

"I'm sure the children won't notice the floral arrangements. They will be too busy playing games and eating the food," Francis protested, but Ellen knew that the children would be escorted by their mothers and she wanted to make a good impression.

Frank had taken to wandering around the house carrying a wooden sword, stabbing at imaginary enemies. His costume was ready, with the red coat and trousers and a hat with a feather. Two of Francis' medals would be attached to his lapel at the last minute.

The day of the party dawned bright and sunny and Clara woke early filled with anticipation at what the day would bring. There were two neatly wrapped parcels on the end of her bed and when she pulled the paper off she found a new frilled dress and an Oriental doll to add to her collection.

Maggie served her favourite breakfast and Francis gave her a stiff hug before returning to the morning paper which he always read very carefully. Ellen was in a cheerful mood and fussed over the flower arrangements as well as going over the party menu once again with Cook.

"It'll be fine, madam. I have prepared this type of food many times. The children will be well fed you can be sure." Cook was used to Ellen's fussy ways and carried on with the preparations for the lunch-time feast.

The morning dragged and then it was time to dress in their costumes and prepare to meet the guests. Esther Jones was first to arrive. She had left the youngest child back with her maid but the others were dressed in a haphazard assortment of clothing making it hard to guess what they actually represented.

"I'm a pirate. I sail on the high seas." "I'm a slave and I was captured by the bad people." They all had wild imaginations and Esther smiled as she saw Clara's costume and admired the painted head band. She was interested to learn that Clara had attended school with her Maori friends and was quite at home wearing their clothing.

By now the other girls were beginning to arrive, all dressed very ornately with colourful costumes complete with many ribbons and bows in their hair. Ellen felt like apologizing for Clara's choice, but held her tongue and welcomed each arrival.

Clara was kept busy opening the parcels and stacking the paper carefully in a corner. What an exciting day she was having. Once the guests had all arrived, Maggie called them outside and organized a game of 'pass the parcel'. Each time she rang the bell the parcel stopped being handed on and a layer of paper was unwrapped. As the last piece fell away, a delighted Frank was left clutching a small coloured ball.

Now it was time for the magician to entertain them and they all trooped back into the living room where a man waited, dressed in a garish suit of shiny purple cloth. He wore a top hat and had a large twirled moustache, making him look a little bit fearsome, Ellen thought.

She held little William who was most intrigued and even Walter's small son Charles was enthralled at the tricks being played out in front of his eyes. The magician made cards disappear and then he retrieved them from someone's ear. He had a small black rabbit that lived in his top hat and a white dove that landed on one of the picture rails, much to the amusement of the children.

After a time, the magician finished with a flourish and enticed the dove down from the picture rail. The children applauded loudly and then it was time for a late lunch. Cook and Maggie had been very busy and the food was temptingly displayed. Most of the children had shed part of their costumes by now, finding them too cumbersome to play in, but Clara remained cool and comfortable, her hair braided in one long plait down her back.

Sandwiches and small pies were soon disappearing, then the cakes and biscuits were brought out. Glasses of lemonade were consumed and a pile of hand-made chocolates left all the faces and hands sticky, until Maggie produced a tub of warm water and some cloths and rapidly cleaned them up.

Clara looked around. Her father had disappeared some time ago and she was disappointed that he wasn't around to share in the feast. He had been watching the magician and then disappeared before the programme had finished. She knew he was not really used to children, but hoped he hadn't gone to his club to get some peace and quiet.

Several of the mothers had arrived to collect their daughters and Frank had finally taken off his hat and laid down his sword. Clara decided to change into something more comfortable, when Ellen called out to her. "Clara, come out here and see what has arrived."

Clara pulled on a simple skirt and thin blouse and picked up a pair of shoes. What could Ellen want? She climbed down the steps to the front yard and looked around. Nothing here, except some of the children playing around as they waited for their mothers. Ellen was standing by the hedge that separated the garden from the small field where her father's horse often grazed and she called out again to Clara.

"Come and see what is by the stable. Your father has a surprise for you."

Clara pulled the gate open and stared towards the stable. Tied up to the rail was the most beautiful pony she had ever seen. He was shiny black with a white blaze on his face and one white sock.

"Go and meet your new pony, Clara. Your father has bought him for you." Ellen beamed as she knew that the girl would be overjoyed at the gift. It warmed her heart to be part of this happy scene.

Francis was standing beside the pony, waiting for Clara to respond. He had ridden quite a distance to collect the pony and had led it back from his own horse. So far, the animal had been well behaved and he liked what he saw.

Clara's hand flew to her mouth. She could not believe she had her very own pony. Unbelievingly, she walked slowly towards her father who held the reins in his hand.

"Come on Clara. This handsome animal is named Beauty and I'm sure you will become great friends." The pony turned and eyed Clara as she walked towards him. She patted his neck and accepted the reins from her father.

"You had better change into your riding habit and then you can try him out," Ellen called from the gate where she was still standing, holding William by the hand as he tugged and tried to follow Clara into the field.

Clara handed the reins back to her father and gave him a huge hug around the neck. "Thank you, father. This is the best day of my life." She scampered back into the house, her guests forgotten in her haste. A few minutes later she was back, dressed in her riding outfit, a whip tucked under her arm.

Her friends watched in envy as she swung onto the saddle and gathered up the reins. The pony responded instantly as she urged him forward with her legs and he walked briskly towards the far end of the field. "He's not a bit like lazy little Whiskey," she called out in delight, as she trotted back to where her father was standing.

"We will ride together tomorrow," her father promised. "For now, you can ride him in the small field and get to know him better."

Francis was confident that his daughter could control the new pony. She was obviously a more experienced rider than he had imagined. Living in the backblocks of Auckland had taught her many skills, that was most obvious.

Chapter 12

Since the visit to Waipuna, both Francis Worrell and Barbara were feeling anxious and unsettled. No business was coming their way and their finances were being increasingly stretched as they had mortgages to manage and debts to repay. The only bright spot on the horizon was the sale of the Takapuna property which had yielded enough funds to service the bulk of their creditors.

"It seems such a shame to let that land go. I know that Takapuna and the whole of the area over the water will be very valuable some day." Francis still had visions of a bridge which would cross the harbour at the narrowest point or a more efficient ferry service.

"At least we are able to settle the most pressing of our debts, but I'm worried about our future here in Auckland." Barbara was philosophical. She had been in this situation a number of times since their marriage all those years ago in London. Francis was always so unpredictable, but she loved him dearly and often said that after more than 40 years it was without one day's regret.

Her patience had been tried many times, however, as Francis' grand schemes so often came to nothing. His father William had been a great scholar as well as a composer and mathematician who had married into a wealthy family which owned considerable property.

William Stevens had also been a contemporary of the Rev Samuel Wesley who ran a church at Epworth, assisted by his wife Susannah. Francis could recall visiting the Wesley household, which was run by Susannah, who also looked after their 19 children and was often left to manage the parish as well as the large garden.

His father and Samuel Wesley would have many a long, earnest discussion about theology as well as sharing a love of poetry and music, while Francis played with the numerous children, including Charles and John who later became famous as church leaders and hymn writers.

Francis still owned a copy of a book written by his father, entitled 'The Circle and the Square in Composition: Or the Quadrature of the Circle', but admitted he had never really understood a word of it.

Yes, Francis had not only inherited his father's intelligence, but also his impractical traits.

They had checked out the living situation of Jane and her children, and found that they were in safe hands with Jane's sister Sophia in their comfortable home in Hobson Bay.

Barbara's thoughts were interrupted by the sound of the mail being dropped into the box. Receiving mail made her feel nervous these days in case there were any more unexpected bills or letters from lawyers. She was pleased to find the letter they had been expecting from young Francis in Wellington. He may have a solution to their problems.

The contents of the letter were very much as Barbara had expected. Francis and Ellen were concerned about their financial situation and sorry that they had given up their Grafton mansion. "Walter and I are most willing to help you in any way we can. We feel that you should finalise your Auckland affairs and move to Wellington where you would be close to more members of your family," Francis wrote.

There was news of the children and a description of the new house which was under construction. The best news of all was the announcement of Ellen's latest pregnancy.

"Look at this, Francis. Ellen is with child again. We will soon be welcoming another grandchild." Francis took the letter and read it through.

"That is great news. But our son is right. It is time to move from Auckland, but I have been thinking about going as far as Dunedin which is a very financial town right now, with much wealth coming from the gold fields. With my experience in mining shares I would have no problem finding employment there."

Barbara considered the idea for a moment. She felt that Wellington would be a more practical choice but Francis was right. He would have no trouble finding work in Dunedin. "I'll leave the decision up to you, my dear. But in the meantime we may as well take down the real estate sign and make an announcement in the newspaper to say the business has been closed."

Francis sighed as he put the letter down. He was always upset when a business venture failed, but normally bounced back quickly. This time it was going to take a little longer.

It took less than a month for Francis and Barbara to settle their affairs in Auckland. They sold the rest of their furniture and felt almost light-hearted as they set off for the South Island with little apart from their clothing and a few pounds in their bank account.

As the ship left the docks in Auckland, Francis held Barbara in his arms and thanked her for showing faith in him. "Most women would have given up on me long ago, but you have remained a faithful wife. I think we will be very happy in our new location."

Barbara smiled. Francis seemed like his old self again and while they had good health and each other, nothing else really mattered. "You are right my dear. I welcome a fresh new start and I know we are ready for a new challenge."

As they watched the shore disappear from the comfort of the ship's lounge, Francis ordered drinks and soon they were sharing stories with the other passengers as they steamed along the east coast towards the Coromandel. Last time she had made this journey, Barbara had been alone but now she was enjoying the experience with her beloved husband.

"It is so much better with you beside me. When we arrive in Dunedin we will set up a new home and buy everything we need." They knew they were heading into cruel winter conditions but were ready to face that problem when they got there.

Soon it was time to retire to their cabin and fall asleep on the narrow bunks. At least there was a bathroom a little way down the hallway, even though it was shared by several other passengers.

Francis woke early and was soon pacing the deck as they entered the harbour at Coromandel. If he looked carefully he could make out the premises on the waterfront that he had shared with his sons at the height of the gold mining bonanza.

A few passengers left the ship and several others joined and by mid day they were ready to continue their journey along the east coast to Tauranga. They were close enough to the shore to observe the mountains and green forests that lined the coast and at times they were escorted by whales and dolphins as they made their way south.

They were blessed with calm weather as they journeyed down the coast towards Wellington. The ship would be in port there for a full day and Francis hoped that his sons would be able to meet them and share their news before they crossed the treacherous strait to the South Island.

It was blowing a gale as they entered the harbour and the tug had difficulty escorting them to the jetty. Francis knew that his son was probably watching from the comfort of his home as the ship battled against the swirl until it finally reached the safety of its mooring.

"We could have stayed with Walter or Francis but I want us to get settled in Dunedin." Francis was anxious to find work and somewhere to live as soon as possible. They only had a few pounds left to their name and he needed to start earning a living as soon as possible.

"I do hope the family can get down to the wharf to meet us. I would love to see the children while we are here." Barbara scanned the crowd standing on the jetty as the ship berthed. Everybody was wrapped up in warm coats and hats to keep out the chill.

As the day was cold they decided to stay on board unless they caught sight of one of their sons. There was no point in getting chilled and the ride in a hired carriage would be an uncomfortable one.

They were just about to give up hope when Francis caught sight of Walter standing on the end of the pier. He leant over the side of the ship and waved vigorously. Walter saw him at once and returned the greeting.

"I'll fetch my hat and meet Walter on the pier. Then I will let you know what has been planned." Francis was off before Barbara had time to answer. She waved to Walter and pointed to the gangway.

Soon the two men were embracing each other and after a few moments Francis beckoned to Barbara to come down and join them. She was already dressed in her warmest coat and scarf so she wasted no time in making her way down the gangway and onto the wharf.

A crew member was standing by and waved to her. "Don't be late getting back. We sail at five o'clock on the dot," he said, as he helped her step down onto the pier.

"We'll be on time," she smiled. "Our son is here to meet us, but we won't be away too long."

Walter stood, tall and elegant in his fine wool coat and trousers. He wore a bowler hat and a silk scarf which completed the picture. "It is so good to see you again Mother. We will go to the tea house a little way from here and Francis is planning to meet us there. We both managed to leave work for a couple of hours but sadly, there won't be time to bring the women and children to see you."

Barbara knew that both her sons had important positions with the Government and could not be away from their desks too long.

"That will be most pleasant. My legs feel as though they are made from rubber after so long on the ship. It is good to walk on firm ground again."

The tea house was a short stroll up from the jetty and they were soon settled around a table set with a white cloth and shining silverware. A few minutes later, Francis walked through the doorway and looked around for them.

It had been some time since he had seen his father and he was surprised at the change in his appearance. His hair was now quite white and his face more lined than before. Obviously, these recent problems were taking their toll on his health. He was pleased to see that his mother looked well and soon they were chatting and catching up on all the latest news.

"We are so pleased that Ellen is with child again. She seems to be coping well with all the children."

"She is not totally comfortable with the children, but nor am I. Luckily they are well behaved and we have plenty of help from our maids." Francis went on to tell his parents about the birthday party and the surprise gift to Clara. "She rides that pony at every opportunity and accompanies me at times, which is most pleasant."

After eating a delicious lunch, Walter and Francis left their parents to make their way back to the ship. The weather was cool and cloudy so they were not tempted to walk around the town and check out the new stores. There would be plenty of time for that when they reached Dunedin.

Chapter 13

Ellen was sorry that she had missed Francis' parents at the waterfront. She could have taken a carriage to get there but gale force winds were threatening and the ride along the waterfront would not have been pleasant.

Although she was feeling well and had overcome the miseries of sickness she was not ready to take any risks. At her age a precious child was at stake and she wanted to deliver another healthy baby to make up for the two children that Francis had already lost.

The new pony had proved to be a great success and now Clara was out riding at every opportunity and spending precious time with the father she had hardly known until a short time ago.

The new house was nearing completion and Ellen was looking forward to letting it out to a person who would possibly provide rooms for well educated young women who were working in the flourishing town.

She was sorry that Francis and Barbara were not settling in Wellington. She knew from past experience what the winters were like in the southern part of the country. Her family had battled many a winter in Southland and she would not want to be back living under those conditions. The windy nature of Wellington was bad enough but at least they didn't have to cope with blizzards and snow for much of the winter.

But now she had other things to think about. It seemed that Maggie, her loyal maid, was about to marry her boyfriend George and move to the Jones' household. That would mean hiring a new girl to fill the position and with a new baby coming soon, Ellen was anxious to find the right person as soon as possible.

Why did life have to be so complicated? The new lass Annie was assisting the cook and coping with the housework but Ellen could not imagine how she, herself, would look after four children without excellent hired help.

Francis consoled her. "Maybe we should hire a woman who is trained to take care of children. I'm sure a good person could be found who would love to live in our comfortable household."

"I do hope so. Maggie has given her notice and although I wish her well, I am most loathe to see her go. I will place an advertisement in the newspaper and see what sort of response we get." Ellen was not so sure. Although she enjoyed the children in small doses, she would not want to be responsible for them day and night.

Francis was pleased that his parents appeared confident about making a new life in Dunedin. He was shocked that his father had aged so much but knew that there were many opportunities in the southern city for someone with his experience.

In the meantime, his work was keeping him busy. The provinces were to be abolished and soon the whole country would be run by the colonial government. With this in mind, a grand building had been commissioned to house the civil service and Francis knew that he and his colleagues would be moving into the Neo-Renaissance style structure over the next few weeks.

Francis could see the merits in abolishing the provincial governments as the provinces had vastly different practices which affected land sales, schooling and charitable aid schemes. Several of the provinces had been forced to borrow from the colonial government when it became obvious that they could not raise sufficient revenue to fund their own programmes.

"The Legislative Council is more trouble than it is worth. Some of those gentlemen have held office for too many years and their ideas are not keeping up with the times," he declared, as he read the daily paper one evening. "The House of Lords may work back in England, but it is not necessary in this young country."

"I don't know, Francis. A second opinion may stop unsuitable bills being passed." Ellen was more conservative about the old ways.

"Poppycock. They just like to hear the sound of their own voices and hold up many good ideas." Francis had experienced many frustrating delays in the settlement of land deals, due to the long-winded nature of the Legislative Council.

Ellen walked from the room. She was feeling restless and uncomfortable with the weight of her unborn child restricting her activities. Thank goodness the baby would be born in a few weeks' time and after that she would feel more like taking up her social activities. Clara's birthday party had been a happy occasion but she had not felt like organising any events since then. She had been invited to attend a number of pleasant afternoon functions, however, and knew she would need to take her turn again soon.

As it turned out, a new woman was found quite quickly to replace young Maggie and she seemed to be capable enough with the younger children. Clara had not really taken to her as she missed Maggie's company and Mrs

Adams was quite strict and did not have the same sense of humour.

Thank goodness for the new pony that occupied most of Clara's spare time. Beauty was proving to be very reliable and she could ride him alone all the way past the tea rooms to the end of the beach where the gravel road ended.

Mrs Adams occasionally walked the children down to the beach where they splashed around in a shallow pool of water. "You will be able to swim when the weather is warmer," she promised, as she wrapped everyone up in warm jackets to keep out the worst of the wind.

There had been no word from Francis' parents but Ellen was not too concerned. "No news is good news," she had said to Francis earlier that day. They would soon hear if there was any problem.

Little William had just woken up from his nap and Ellen took him from Mrs Adams and sat down with him in a comfortable chair in the small sitting room.   The walls were lined with book cases and a narrow casement window offered a glimpse of the bay and distant town beyond.

Mrs Adams planned to take the two youngest children for a stroll along the parade, with William wrapped up in the large perambulator and Frank following along behind. Clara was due home from school at any time.

"You really are growing into a big boy, William. You are really too large for the buggy now and your new brother or sister will be able to use it." Ellen smiled at her small son who studied her with his bright blue eyes.

He was soon anxious to be on the move and waddled away on his fat little legs, waving to Ellen as he followed Mrs Adams into the nursery.

Frank was impatient to be on their way and Ellen looked at him and sighed. "You are six years old now, Frank. Your father wants you to start school as soon as the weather improves. You will go with Clara to the Te Aro School which is not too far from here." Ellen knew that the school, which was situated close to their previous home in Ghuznee Street near St Peter's Church, had a good reputation and Clara was happy there.

There were plans to move the school into a new building but that was a year or two away. There was still no necessity to send children to school but Francis predicted that an Act would be passed in the near future, making schooling compulsory for all children.

Frank was already learning his letters and could write his name. Maggie had turned learning into a game whenever she could and Ellen hoped the new nurse maid would do the same.

She was pleased to lie down and take a short nap once the children left the house. Her ankles were swollen and she was relieved to take the weight off her feet. Being with child was not a pleasant experience.

A few days after Francis and Barbara landed in Dunedin they met with good fortune. Francis walked into a small, dark tavern and the first person he saw was an old acquaintance from Auckland who greeted him with open arms.

"Francis Stevens, what are you doing so far south? I thought you were comfortably entrenched in the warmth of the north." George Moore clasped Francis' hand and shook it firmly.

"It's good to see you George. I am hoping to settle in this fine town and see what good fortune comes my way." Francis allowed himself to be led to a wooden booth with a long table and bench seats.

"You could do worse than Dunedin. The gold has been bringing great wealth to these parts. Although the claims are coming in more slowly now there is still plenty of work for an experienced man like you."

Francis settled with a drink and listened to what his old friend had to say. "I will put in a good word for you at the assayers' office where they need men to accept the samples from the prospectors."

Although Francis had not experienced this side of the business he thought he would be able to talk to the men and keep records of what was brought in to be analyzed. His son Sydney would have been better equipped for the job but he was now back with the postal service.

"That sounds very promising. I have closed my share broking business and no longer wish to deal with real estate. An assayers' office could be very interesting." Francis emptied his glass and it was promptly refilled with rich frothy beer.

"I hope you like our Dunedin brew. It is very popular around these parts." George finished his drink and filled his glass from the jug which had been placed on the table.

Francis looked around him. The conversation flowed and the accents were thick, mostly Scottish, with many new arrivals from the old country. It was a totally different world from Auckland where he had enjoyed the company of English gentlemen, rather than burly gold diggers and labourers.

He and Barbara had rented a furnished property in Dunedin's steepest street and Barbara was kept busy stoking the fires to keep the house warm. The first snow had already fallen and this was a new experience for both of them.

At first they were entranced as the countryside turned white and the trees stood like ghosts in the gloomy landscape. But the novelty soon wore off as the snow melted and turned to brown sludge.

Francis was filled with optimism as he made his way back to where Barbara was waiting. She was anxious to hear how his enquiries had gone and was relieved at the news of a possible job opportunity. She had prepared a simple meal and they ate it in front of a blazing fire in the sitting room. A second fire had been lit in the bedroom and stacked with slow burning coals to warm the room ready for the night.

"I have filled copper pans with hot water and placed them in our bed. We will have warm feet for a short time at least." Barbara was adapting quickly to the new environment.

"I must admit I will be happier when the warmer weather comes. This dampness is getting into my joints and I swear I have aged 10 years since we arrived." Francis pulled his chair closer to the fire. "You have made the house very cosy, my love, and I feel that we will soon adjust to this new lifestyle."

Chapter 14

The gardens were bright with spring flowers when John Stevens came into the world on a bright sunny morning. Ellen's labour had been mercifully quick this time and she sat up in bed in the comfortable nursing home waiting for her husband to visit.

Francis was full of smiles as he came through the door, carrying a large bouquet of flowers which he placed on the cabinet beside the bed. "You look very well my dear. I think childbirth becomes you."

Ellen grimaced at the thought of any more confinements. From now on Francis would have to be very careful as she was determined that this newest child would be her last.

"Have you seen your little boy yet?" she asked. "He is every bit as handsome as young William but a little heavier I believe."

Francis admitted that he had been shown the baby through the glass which separated the nursery from the corridor. He had been wrapped up tightly with just the top of his head showing. One baby looked much like another as far as he was concerned.

"I feel very fortunate to have four healthy children. Mrs Adams will bring the family in to see their new brother in a few days' time. In the meantime, I need to get back to the office. Now we have moved into the new building it is taking some time to adjust. It is really very ornate and I will take you to visit it once you are home and rested."

Francis gave Ellen a quick peck on the cheek and picked up his hat. "I will see you again this evening. In the meantime have a good rest." Ellen waved her hand, then settled back and closed her eyes. She knew the babies would be brought out to be fed in a few hours and she was happy to rest her aching body.

A white-gowned nurse bustled in and straightened the bedcovers. She picked up the flowers and took them away to be placed in a vase. "Just ring the bell if you need anything, my dear," she said as she left the room. "In the meantime take the opportunity to rest."

Back at Oriental Bay, Clara was testing the patience of the new nurse maid. She wanted to go out and ride her pony but Mrs Adams insisted that she tidy her room first. "I thought that was the maid's job. Father and Ellen never make me clean my room."

"Then it's high time you learned. You may not always be in a position to hire staff and a lady needs to learn how to run a household." Mrs Adams was insistent. "There will be plenty of time to ride your pony when you have finished."

Clara set about the task as quickly as she could. Her dresses were hung in the wardrobe and the doll collection was straightened. She changed into her outdoor clothes and was soon on her way to the stable where Beauty would be waiting.

It didn't take long to gear up the pony and climb onto the saddle. The air was fresh and clear and the wind had dropped so the ride along the water front was most pleasant. The narrow track avoided the worst of the rocks and marshland and soon she was trotting along a firm stretch of sand at the far end of the beach.

Suddenly a horse and cart rattled around a bend and Beauty shied in terror. Before she knew it Clara was hurled through the air and landed on a rocky ledge, her arm bent at an awkward angle. She managed to keep hold of the reins with her other hand and Beauty came to a halt, his eyes wide with fright.

Clara tried to stand but the pain in her arm forced her to stay where she was. Luckily a man and woman were walking along the track and they hurried towards her. "Are you alright?" the woman asked, but she could see from the look on Clara's face that she was in trouble. The man took the reins from Clara and the woman helped her to her feet, but she clung to her useless arm which was obviously badly injured.

"We must get you to a doctor. I think your arm might be broken." The woman looked most concerned.

The driver of the horse and cart had also seen Clara fall and after tying his horse to a fence he came over to investigate. "I will drive you home and then your family can get you to a doctor." Between them they lifted Clara onto the cart and tied the pony to a rail on the side.

A few moments later they reached the Stevens' home and Mrs Adams came hurrying out. "What has happened? Are you alright?" She soon took in the situation as a white-faced Clara was helped down from the cart.

"Oh, my dear child. Come inside and we will summon a doctor at once." Mrs Adams thanked the carriage driver and escorted Clara into the house. She wrapped a firm bandage around the damaged arm and sat Clara in a chair.

The groundsman had come in to see what all the fuss was about and a few minutes later he instructed his young assistant, Robert, to ride the pony to the doctor's office on the edge of town.

Clara was doing her best not to cry although her arm throbbed and her knee was grazed. "It wasn't Beauty's fault. He got a fright when the cart came around the corner."

"No-one will blame the animal. It was just an unlucky accident and soon you will feel much better." Mrs Adams had lost her stern look as she tended to Clara and made her comfortable.

A whole hour went by before the doctor arrived, astride a large black horse. He carried a brown bag and smiled kindly at Clara. "Let me take a look at that arm, my dear. Can you move it at all?"

Clara tried to move the arm without much success and the pain was so severe it brought tears to her eyes. "Will I need to go to the hospital? My father and Ellen will be worried about me."

"We will take care of everything. Just be brave and keep your arm as still as you can." The doctor re-bandaged the arm and tied a sling around Clara's neck. "That will keep your arm still and prevent it from receiving more damage. We may need to put you to sleep for a short time to set the arm if the bone is broken."

After riding the short distance to the doctor's office, Robert then headed along the waterfront until he came to the new Government building in Beach Street on Lambton Quay. He was enjoying the opportunity to ride the pony that he often fed and groomed when Clara was busy with her schooling.

He was conscious of his shabby clothing when he turned into the grounds of the Government Building. The sight of the four-storied wooden ediface took his breath away.

Although it was built from Kauri, it resembled an Italian stone palace and he had been told that it was easiest the largest building in the country. There were many well-dressed gentlemen standing in groups, deep in conversation and he felt a little shy as he approached them.

"I have an urgent message for Mr Francis Stevens. Would you be able to find him and tell him that Robert is here?"

"I know Mr Stevens well. Is there a problem with his wife or the new child?" One of the men looked concerned. He didn't want to be the deliverer of bad news."

Robert hesitated for a moment. "No. Mrs Stevens is well. It is his daughter Clara who has injured her arm and needs to go to the hospital."

"It may take me some time to locate Mr Stevens, but I will send him out. You should take the opportunity to water your pony as he seems to have travelled some distance." The man disappeared inside the building and Robert dismounted and led Beauty to the concrete drinking trough.

The scene was a busy one as furniture, books and documents were being unloaded from carts and taken into the new building. The civil servants would certainly have a great view over the bustling waterfront to the harbour beyond.

It wasn't long before Francis Stevens came into sight as he walked quickly down the stone steps and onto the drive way. Robert waved his hand and led Beauty towards him.

"What has happened to Clara? Has she been badly injured?"

"Her pony took fright at a noisy cart and Clara was tossed from the saddle. The doctor has seen her and wants her to go to the hospital to check out her arm as it might be broken."

"Then I will get my horse and come home at once. You had better ride ahead as I will have to arrange for a comfortable carriage for the journey. The hospital is just a short distance from here but quite a ride from Oriental Bay I'm afraid."

Back at their home Clara was settled on a comfortable couch wrapped up in a warm blanket. The doctor had advised Mrs Adams to give her a cup of warm, sweet tea but no food in case chloroform had to be used.

"Your father should be home shortly and he can accompany you to the hospital. I need to stay here with your two brothers who will be demanding lunch before too long."

Clara lay and thought about what had happened. She loved her pony and knew that it was out of character for him to shy. She wondered when she would be able to ride him again. Mrs Adams had been treating her ever so kindly since she had been delivered home so perhaps she should start being nicer to her.

Her thoughts were interrupted when she heard the front door being closed and her father came striding into the room. He looked so concerned it would have been almost funny if her arm wasn't hurting so badly.

"It's okay. It's only my arm and it wasn't Beauty's fault," she burst out. The tears, which she had managed to hold back until now, tumbled onto her cheeks and she angrily wiped them away.

"The carriage will be here any moment to take you to the hospital. I will have to ride along behind so I can get home later." Francis was relieved that his daughter looked reasonable healthy. Her arm would soon heal and there did not appear to be any other damage.

They didn't have long to wait before two men came into the room carrying a stretcher. Clara looked at it in dismay. She could easily walk out to the carriage but much to her embarrassment they insisted on carrying her.

The stretcher fitted between the seats of the covered carriage and Clara lay wedged on the narrow bed for the journey to the hospital. One of the men had encouraged her to breathe in some laudanum from a bottle and soon a drowsy feeling came over her and she scarcely felt the pain in her arm.

Soon everything happened through a haze. Being moved onto a bed, wheeled into a bright room, a mask being held over her face and then oblivion.

She woke to find herself in a hospital bed with a rail to keep her from falling out. Her father was sitting on a hard wooden chair beside the bed and a nurse hovered near the doorway. She came over when she saw Clara open her eyes and picked up her wrist to take her pulse.

"Your arm has been plastered to keep it still until the break mends. You will have to keep it dry until the cast comes off in about six weeks," her father said. "The doctor wants you to stay in hospital overnight and I will be here to collect you some time tomorrow."

Francis gave his daughter a quick kiss on the forehead and left. He needed to get back to the office for a meeting and then visit Ellen and the new baby before he could return home. He knew that Mrs Adams would cope with the children back at the house and a meal would be ready for him later that evening. Being a family man was exhausting when you weren't used to it, he decided.

Chapter 15

With the winter weather behind them, Barbara and Francis were enjoying the fresh air and colourful gardens of Dunedin. The garden of their rented house was blooming with a great variety of spring bulbs and Barbara delighted in gathering up a handful of flowers each day and placing them in a vase to brighten up the dining room.

She still lit a fire in the large living area but as the days grew longer the sun warmed the house for much of the time.

Francis had settled into his job at the assayers' office. It was interesting work as miners came in with their rock samples, hoping that enough of the elusive gold ore would be seen, enough to make them wealthy. Once in a while there was great excitement when someone struck a rich seam but mostly it was hard work with little result.

They had paid off the last of their creditors, but apart from two parcels of land in the far north of the country, they owned nothing except the clothes they wore. If only some of Francis' grand ideas had come to fruition they would not be in this position now.

Barbara was philosophical, however. "We always have enough money to survive. We are healthy and happy so what else do we really need?"

"We could be living in a grand mansion with servants and great art works adorning our walls." Francis was becoming eloquent.

"We have done that many times, back in England and also in Auckland. I have no desire to live in a mausoleum surrounded by dreary portraits. I am very happy to be sharing my life with you."

Francis went off next morning feeling satisfied that Barbara was having no regrets. One of the clerks had left an English newspaper on a seat and because he hadn't had any word from his home country for some time, Francis picked it up and scanned the headlines. There was little of interest until he came to a small item near the back of the newspaper.

The inhabitants of Kidderminster were about to erect a statue in honour of Rowland Hill, as the originator of the adhesive and universal penny postage stamp.

Francis stopped in his tracks. He couldn't believe what he was reading. Many years before, while he was a schoolmaster back in Chigwell, he had come up with the idea of a postage stamp and he had sent a letter to Lord Althorp, Chancellor of the Exchequer, with an illustration which used the Royal Arms, rather than the likeness of the reigning monarch, William the Fourth.

Francis had shared the idea with a teacher who worked for a time at the school. Mr Rowland Hill had joined the staff and they had become great friends. He wrote articles for a number of magazines and expressed an interest in writing a pamphlet about the penny postage stamp.

"One evening, after a pleasant chat and a little wine, I lent him the papers and he promised to write the pamphlet and then give it to me for my signature, or cast it in the fire if I didn't like it." Francis was thinking aloud, remembering the occasion well.

He was still angry when he returned home that evening. "Do you remember my submissions on a universal postage stamp?"

"That was many years ago, my dear, but I remember it well. It was going to make you famous but it came to nothing."

"You are not going to believe this. Rowland Hill has claimed the idea as his own and now the town of Kidderminster is erecting a large statue, honouring him as the inventor of the stamp."

"I believe Rowland Hill was knighted for his work for the postal service. The introduction of the postage stamp was merely part of the overall reforms." Barbara had read several accounts of Sir Rowland's progress over the years. Before the introduction of the postal stamp, mail recipients had to pay the postage, based on the number of sheets and how far the mail had to travel. The system was very complicated and expensive as the delivery person had to collect the postage charges.

"The postage stamp was a major part of the reforms. He could at least have acknowledged me as the inventor. Of course I knew about the introduction of the Penny Post but at the time I was too involved with my business affairs to take much notice. Now, the thought of the people of the town paying for a statue really annoys me."

Francis barely slept that night, his mind wrestling with the idea that someone else was being honoured when it should have been him. Apart from the fact that Rowland Hill had used a likeness of Queen Victoria instead of the Royal Arms, the postage stamp was very much like the one that he had designed.

The next day he scoured the papers again and this time there was a major article acknowledging the work of Sir Rowland Hill. He had started work as a schoolmaster and advocated education as a lifelong process, giving children the skills to cope with life, rather than just cramming them with facts.

After successfully introducing the Post Office Reform he became a prominent public figure, a fellow of the Royal Society and was knighted in 1860.

Francis read on. "Illness forced him from his post as Chief Secretary to the Postmaster General in 1864 and Parliament granted him 20,000 pounds and an annual salary of 2000 pounds as a pension."

"Twenty thousand pounds and a substantial pension! I don't begrudge him that good fortune after all the work he has done for the postal service. It is just the erection of a statue in his likeness that has me fuming. I don't want the money. I just want the statue pulled down."

Barbara knew she would get no peace until Francis had got this latest disappointment out of his system. Yes, she did remember the correspondence between her husband and Lord Althorp but like many of Francis' inventions, the idea was not pursued.

"I suggest you write your thoughts down and I will add some ideas of my own. We could send the information to my old friend, the Reverend Rowsell, who is still chaplain to the queen and ask him to convey the message to Her Majesty."

"You do have friends in high places if I recall, but they may not remember us after all this time."

"They would have found it difficult to forget you with all the letters you have sent them over the years. Your ideas for defending the nation must fill many a filing cabinet in the war office by now."

"You are right. All those suggestions and very little reward. But you know I enjoy being an inventor. What comes of the idea doesn't trouble me too much. But I will write a petition about the postage stamp and have it published. I feel it is my duty to make the whole case public."

He stomped away to find some writing paper. He would publish a pamphlet and distribute it around the town. He owed it to his family to have his best idea acknowledged.

Barbara settled down to her needlework. Francis would be happily occupied for many a day finding the letters and recalling the story. She would be surprised if the article ever saw the light of day but she would do what she had promised and write to her former friend.

It had been some time since she had been in touch with Thomas Rowsell, who had been private chaplain to the Royal Family for many years. Indeed, if she had remained in London, instead of in far away New Zealand, she might still be friendly with the family. She would have to remind him that he knew her as Barbara Vickers, and that his sisters were at one time, her very best friends.

But if she had remained in England, Barbara may have lost touch with her former circle of friends, as Thomas' sister Sarah had married England's foremost architect, Sir Charles Barry, and that would probably have taken her right out of Barbara's league. But they had all started off as children at Hornsey and Newington, where they had stayed at each other's homes on many occasions.

Barbara sighed. It would be great to see the name, Francis Worrell Stevens, recognised as the inventor of the postal stamp, even if he received no monetary reward. Yes, she would help her husband in any way she could.

Chapter 16

By the time Francis Stevens left his office it was too late to see Ellen and the newborn child as visiting hours were strictly adhered to. He was able to leave her a note with a promise to visit her the next day. He did not mention Clara's misfortune as there was nothing that Ellen could do for the child.

He rode towards the bay intending to head for his home, but decided to call at the gentlemen's club for a quick drink to celebrate the safe arrival of another son. It would be good to catch up with some of his friends, rather than return home to the company of housekeepers and young children.

The first person he saw was his brother Walter who shook him by the hand when he was told the news. "Well done Francis. A new wife and four children in as many years is quite an accomplishment."

Francis grimaced. "I tell you, having brought all my children together has become a trifle overwhelming. It is just as well we have good help, otherwise neither Ellen nor I would be able to cope."

They sat down for a drink while Francis told his brother about Clara's fall and they shared their thoughts on the move to the new Government building. Several of their fellow workers were also sharing a companionable drink and soon they were all congratulating Francis on his latest son.

Two hours went by before Francis climbed carefully aboard his trusty steed and made his way slowly around the bay to his home. His dinner was being kept warm over a pan of hot water and was served up by an unsmiling maid who was not pleased at having to work late.

There was no sign of Mrs Adams or the children so Francis went straight to his bedroom and climbed into his lonely bed where he instantly fell into an untroubled sleep.

The next few days flew by with Clara being delivered back from the hospital, followed a week later by Ellen and the new child. Francis was kept busy sorting out the mountain of paperwork that had been moved from the old building.

"I'm sure we will never locate many of our own files, let alone the paper work that comes in from the other provinces once the system is centralized." Francis could see many hours of work ahead of him."

His brother agreed. "Most of the provinces voted in favour of amalgamation but Auckland and Dunedin are far from pleased. They were quite content to keep managing their own affairs. It will take some time to sort everything out."

Even the Colonial Treasurer Julius Vogel said: "The provinces have broken down because of their coming into conflict with the colonial government on many points, and especially on matters of finance."

At the time of the recent election a vote had been taken on the abolition of the provinces, returning a majority in favour of abolition. The new Premier, Harry Atkinson, did not take long to announce the changes and the Counties Act was passed which divided the rural parts of the colony into counties.

With the help of Mrs Adams, Ellen was soon up and about, and it wasn't long before she was worried that the baby was not gaining as much weight as he should. "I am not designed to feed babies, I'm afraid," she declared. "We will need to find a wet nurse as I don't have sufficient milk to satisfy him."

"He is a large baby and very hungry. We can supplement the milk with a little thin porridge if you wish, but it might pay to advertise for a suitable person to feed the little boy." Mrs Adams had a wealth of experience in these matters and reassured Ellen that it was not her fault.

She knew that many women hired somebody else to feed a child. It would be a woman who had recently had a baby of her own and enough milk for two infants. Francis felt a little embarrassed as he handed the note to the clerk at the newspaper office. It was not the sort of thing that people talked about and was outside his experience.

"The advertisement will appear in the next newspaper and I hope you get a good response." The young lad tried to keep a straight face.

Francis was once again late in reaching the office but he usually made up for it by working into the evening. The pile of papers on his desk did not seem to be getting any smaller and he knew that he would need another assistant to help him with the backlog.

Since transferring from the Defence Department to become chief clerk of the General Crown Lands Office, he had dealt with the allocation of Crown land for many purposes.

He was particularly involved in the Homestead Settlement scheme in which settlers could be granted a free piece of land which they were required to live on and improve.

"Many people who could never have bought their own land have been assisted in this way," he would explain. "At the same time, large areas of the country have been cleared and are now supporting all types of agriculture."

Ellen could see the value of this, especially in more remote areas, but she would often remember how her own father had arrived from Ireland and bought his large acreage in Southland with no assistance from anyone.

She was only 11 years old at the time but could remember it clearly. Landing in Dunedin and boarding a coach to take them all the way to Invercargill where they lived for a while before a house was built on the land in Southland. She was not too sure about lending a helping hand so readily.

The advertisement brought a number of replies and after Mrs Adams had interviewed the applicants, she chose a young woman who had given birth to a child out of wedlock and needed somewhere to live. The woman was clean and tidy and her situation would remain a secret as long as she stayed in their household.

"I think this young woman will be most suitable. She can share the nursery with the new child at no cost as long as she feeds young John when necessary." Ellen was quite taken with young Mary the moment she set eyes on her and knew all her worries were over when she saw how well she looked after her own child.

Eighteen-year-old Mary had been seduced by an older man but did not want to bring disgrace on her family. They had hidden her during the pregnancy but now that the little girl had been born she needed somewhere to stay until the child was older.

Little John didn't seem to notice the difference when he was first introduced to Mary and latched on hungrily and drank his fill. She smiled as she patted him on the head. "You are a fine little lad and I'm sure we will suit each other well."

The fact that she had such an elegant address to stay in and plenty of food to eat certainly made Mary feel better about her circumstances and she was grateful to Ellen for giving her the chance to raise her daughter in comfort.

A single room was allotted to Mrs Adams and William was moved in to share Frank's bedroom.

With so many women in the house, Francis felt quite overwhelmed and often stopped off at the club for a bit of congenial company. Ellen had made it very clear that any love making was out of the question for some time but he was usually too exhausted to be tempted by the time he arrived home.

Clara was very puzzled about the new arrival in the household, especially when she saw her breast feeding little John. She was getting on much better with Mrs Adams since the accident and since she couldn't ride Beauty for the next few weeks, she spent a lot of time in her company.

Young Frank had been taught his letters and numbers and was now attending the Te Aro School with Clara, who coped the best she could with her injured arm.

Now that she was free from the constraints of feeding her son, Ellen lost no time in getting back into the social life of Wellington. She was pleased with the progress on the new house and supervised the fittings and decoration. It was a very large house of two storeys and boasted an entry hall and ornate staircase which was covered in plush red carpet.

There were several small bedrooms suitable for single women as well as the usual service rooms and two large living areas. This was going to be the most elegant boarding establishment in the whole of Wellington and she would need someone very special to run it.

The elevated location allowed views over the harbour and a small verandah attached to the front of the house offered a panoramic sight over a wide area. Ellen was grateful that the proposed boat slip had not gone ahead and the bay had retained its peaceful outlook.

Now that she owned three large houses in the street, Ellen was keen to give each one a name. "It is so confusing just to allot numbers to the houses. Each one has a personality of its own and I feel that names would be more appropriate."

Francis was too busy to pay much heed to his wife's fanciful ideas, but smiled kindly as she tossed around some names. "The new house will be named Croham, the double villa next door will be Dromahaire and, I know this sounds self indulgent, but I would love to name our own home Ellensville."

"You have chosen names from your home country, Ireland, but as they were built with money which originated from your Irish father, who am I to question your wishes?" Francis was content to go along with the idea if it kept his wife happy. She had provided him with two fine sons and ran the household like clockwork. There was little romance left in their relationship but he found their life together most compatible.

Ellen had recently taken up the game of Bridge and was often away during the day, playing the game and enjoying the afternoon tea supplied. She was careful not to overindulge, however, as she wished to lose weight and regain her former shape.

The day the plaster came off her arm, Clara was so relieved that she threw her arms around Mrs Adams' neck and gave her a hug. Young George had been exercising the pony for the past few weeks and Clara was keen to take over as soon as she could. At first she was a little nervous as her arm had not yet regained its full strength, but with George walking beside her, she walked and trotted around the small field, her confidence soon returning.

Mrs Adams often accompanied her with baby John in the perambulator and William and Frank running ahead as they made their way along the shoreline towards the far end of the bay.

A tenant had been found to run the boarding house and Clara watched curiously as a number of young women, dressed in the most fashionable attire, climbed down from the horse-drawn cabs and walked past their house each evening.

She would love to be old enough to be employed as she found her school lessons boring, apart from the art lessons which she enjoyed,. "I think I will design beautiful dresses and coats and maybe create elegant hats," she told Mrs Adams.

"You show no interest in dressing in fancy clothes yourself. Why would you want to create designs for other people?"

It was true that although Clara preferred simple clothes in plain materials for herself, her imagination ran away with her when she began sketching clothing for others. "Elegant ladies need to showcase their beauty. Maybe when I am older, I will want to wear the latest fashions and colours."

Ellen was also astonished at the creativity in Clara's sketches. Her own dresses were usually very ornate with many yards of material and fine lace trimmings. Although Clara's designs were more simple, she vowed that she would encourage this new interest.

After a number of failed pregnancies, Walter's wife Emily was now conspicuously pregnant and they were confident that this time a live child would be born. Their son Charles was almost eight years old and attended the same school as Clara and Frank. Although he was so young, his father had signed him up with the nearby cricket club and he was already showing an ability to bowl a good length.

When a daughter, Caroline, was born at the start of summer there was much celebration. "We will have to let our parents know as soon as possible. We've hardly heard from them since they moved to Dunedin but I will send a telegraph to inform them of the good news," said Walter.

Like his brother, Walter had been so busy since the move to the new Government Building that he had scarcely had time to worry about his parents. But now he would contact them without delay.

Chapter 17

For many weeks Francis Worrell spent all his spare time working on his petition to send to Her Majesty, Queen Victoria. He had found most of the copies of the original letters and Barbara had written her notes to Rev Rowsell.

The first page stated his intentions very clearly as it read: "Rowland Hill not the originator of the Penny Postage Stamp but Francis Worrell Stevens, formerly of Loughton, Essex, England and now of Dunedin, New Zealand, is the inventor of the adhesive and universal penny postage stamp."

He described how he had submitted the important measure of a postage stamp to Lord Althorp and received a letter in return from his secretary acknowledging the correspondence, copies of which should be available in Downing Street.

He went on to outline his family history and describe the time he was running the school at Loughton which he inherited from his father. He talked about employing Rowland Hill to teach at his school and how they enjoyed each other's company during the evenings.

"My assistant Rowland Hill used to wear a long black coat and his hair was very long, and in the mornings he would take the boys for a run along the gladeway in the forest, and he invariably went without his hat. I was much amused to see his long hair and coat tails flying as he rushed along in front of the boys."

Francis went on to say that he had recently heard that Rowland Hill had been given a substantial reward and a memorial was to be erected in his former town. "Whenever the name of Rowland Hill was mentioned in my presence as the originator of the Penny Postage system I have always contradicted it, and my family and friends are well aware of the fact."

The pamphlet now covered 12 pages and Francis was ready to take it to the printer. He would order enough to be distributed around the major towns in New Zealand and a few would be sent to newspapers in England.

"There. I am satisfied that I have done all I can." Francis sat back and relaxed for the first time in weeks. "Now let us have a drink together to celebrate the completion of the project."

There was a knock on the door at that moment and next thing, Francis came back with a telegraph in his hand. Barbara reached out to take the document, hoping that it would not contain bad news.

"Walter and Emily have a healthy daughter. That is really worth celebrating. Young Charles has got a sister at last."

"That calls for a double celebration. Unfortunately we have no family close by to join us. We really must pay them a visit as soon as possible to see the new grandchildren." Barbara was conscious that all the ones she loved were indeed a long distance away. How good it would be to see one of them now to share the news.'

The pamphlets were printed and dispatched and it wasn't long before an article appeared in the Otago Daily Times, commenting on the story. "Sir Rowland Hill's claim to be regarded as the author of the penny postage system of Great Britain is contested very strongly by a gentleman who lived formerly in Essex, England," it read. "Francis Worrell Stevens, now residing in Dunedin, thinks he is fairly entitled to claim some recognition of his efforts as the real suggestor of a system which has proved to be so beneficial in every respect."

There was much debate around the town for a week or two and then the whole subject was forgotten. So far, there had been no word from the Rev Rowsell or Her Majesty, Queen Victoria.

Now that he had published his pamphlet, Francis appeared to be satisfied. He had told his story and that was all that mattered. It was time to devote his energies to something else.

The opportunity to catch up with their family came from an unexpected source. Their son Sydney announced that he and his fiancé Annie Foster were to be married in Invercargill which was not a great distance from Dunedin by coastal steamer. Sydney's job with the postal service had taken him to several locations around New Zealand and for a time, Invercargill would be their home.

The marriage of Sydney and Annie was indeed a great occasion. As the bride's family lived in Tasmania and couldn't make the journey, the number of guests was small, but Sydney's family was well represented.

His parents sat proudly in the front pew of the small church, Francis in an immaculate coat with tails and carrying a top hat. Barbara was elegantly dressed in dark blue silk with a large feathered hat.

Sydney was surprised at the last minute appearance of his brothers. Francis and Walter caught up with him as he was about to enter the church. They clasped hands as they wished him well in his marriage.

"I can't wait to introduce you to my beautiful Annie. She is truly a delightful lady."

The small crowd waited expectantly until the organ played and the bride, wearing a simple lace gown, was escorted down the aisle by Sydney's employer, who had become a close friend.

As they turned to see their future daughter-in-law for the first time, Francis and Barbara felt very proud. There may have been many highs and lows in their lives, but they had raised their sons well. Francis grasped Barbara's hand tightly and whispered loudly in her ear. "It is grand to see our sons together. I know that the future of the Stevens' family is in good hands."

Chapter 18, 1890s

Oriental Bay was at its pristine best as Francis and Ellen Stevens strolled across the road to the waterfront. Francis had arranged for many yards of sand to be deposited along the shoreline from the ballast of ships which entered the harbour and the beach had become a favourite destination for family groups.

"We have no worries over finance thanks to your father's latest bequest. Five hundred pounds is no mean sum."

"We are very fortunate that my father was able to gift us all such a generous amount even though most of his properties are still to be sold. Luckily, the returns from the rental properties fund the mortgage payments, but there are rumours that the Bank of New Zealand may be in trouble. We have funds with them that could be in danger if that ever happened."

Ellen had invested wisely and now owned four properties in Hay Street, as well as Ellensville, the large home on the corner where they still lived. Wellington had surpassed Dunedin as the financial capital of New Zealand and many major finance companies had set up in the town.

Many of the early wooden buildings had been replaced by more substantial structures of brick and mortar and grand homes for merchants and politicians had been built on the hills behind the town.

"Wellington is in the mood for celebrating. We will all be taking part in the grand parade next weekend. William and John are quite excited about it."

The family had been invited to join the parade of carriages to mark Wellington's 50th anniversary. Although the boys were now teenagers they were still eager to be part of the parade.

Over the years, Clara had returned several times to Mauku where her grandparents were still farming. On one of these visits she was introduced to a young man named William who farmed a property on the west coast near Raglan. It was a difficult romance as they lived so many miles apart, but their friendship grew and Clara declared her love for him.

William's first wife had died, leaving him with three young daughters and Ellen was at first taken aback at the idea that Clara, who was used to a comfortable life in Wellington, should contemplate living in the back of beyond.

"She will be taking on a husband and a ready made family. I hope she realizes what she is doing."

Francis looked at his wife with a wry smile. "Didn't you do the same thing yourself, all those years ago?"

"Yes. But that was different. We lived in a very comfortable home and there was always plenty of household help. It is a totally different situation."

Clara just smiled at Ellen's concerns. "I grew up on a farm so life in the country will be no hardship for me. Besides, I love William and know he will make me very happy."

The marriage was arranged for August, almost eight months away, and Clara would spend the time between her father's and grandparents' homes. She had left school as soon as possible and taken up employment in a drapery store helping fashionable ladies choose the right accessories. She had also become interested in the Suffrage movement and attended many meetings to promote votes for women.

Her own taste in clothing hadn't changed greatly and she would often try to encourage Ellen to dress a little less formally. Ellen, however, believed in dressing up for dinner every night, mainly in long black skirts and ornate blouses, as well as beautiful jewellery.

"We need to maintain a certain standard," she would say.

The day of the parade, Clara and her friends assembled on the pavement to watch the action. The streets had been brightly decorated and there was a surge of excitement as the sound of fife and drum bands could be heard. Soon the colourful marchers came into view, followed by hundreds of school children, each carrying a flag or ribbon, which they waved enthusiastically in the air.

Clara was glad she had worn flat soled shoes, as it took almost an hour for the parade to pass. Carriage after carriage rolled by, with every notable citizen in the town having been invited. Maori dignitaries were included, as well as many of the earliest settlers.

She waved and cheered as her father's carriage came into sight, with Ellen and her two brothers leaning out to catch a glimpse of her. What a wonderful celebration of the day the first settlers landed at Petone back in 1840.

As the parade passed, the crowds gradually moved away leaving a sea of paper behind, to be picked up and tossed around by the wind which blew strongly.

Clara and her friends gathered in one of the many tea houses along Courtney Place and the rest of the afternoon passed happily. "I will miss all this excitement when I am out in the hills with nothing but trees and sheep to look at."

She felt a moment of sadness that her life would change so much.

"But you will be so busy with a new husband and his children to take care of. You won't have time to be gazing at the trees." Her friends loved to tease her about her engagement to a far away suitor.

As Ellen rode in the carriage through the crowded streets she had time to reflect on the many changes that had taken place in the time that she had lived there. From a raw colonial town, Wellington had developed into the colony's centre of power and influence. It was the hub of national trade and the port was now the busiest in the country.

There were many happy memories as the children grew up and developed their interests. Francis' eldest son Frank had moved to Western Australia where he had taken up a secretarial post with the government. He had returned briefly to marry Edith Everill, who had recently arrived from Croyden, Surrey. As neither of Edith's parents was in New Zealand, Ellen acted as hostess for the reception which was held at their home.

"What a great occasion that was," Ellen remembered. "Such a pretty bride with her handsome dress of ivory satin and the dear little attendants, all resplendent in white muslin." She recalled the pretty bonnets and the baskets of flowers they carried. There were many fine gifts from China and England which all had to be transported across the Tasman to where the couple was setting up their home.

William and John were top students at Wellington College and there were high hopes for their future. They both excelled at sports and Francis often spent a day watching cricket or rugby, as his sons did their best to perform well.

"Our sons are high achievers. They seem intent on outdoing each other." Ellen sometimes worried that the boys were a little too competitive.

"The colony is developing fast and there are many talented people moving here. With that competitive nature they will do well in whatever career they choose."

Francis was due to retire in two years and was in a position to observe the many changes taking place within the Government. For the first time, there were to be two parties contesting the General Election. A new Liberal Party, led by the charismatic John Ballance, was to contest the seats at the General Election later in the year.

Up until that time the seats had been held by Independents with no party affiliation.

With the Suffrage Movement being so strong, Francis knew it wouldn't be long before a petition would be presented calling on Parliament to grant the vote to women.

This was a hot topic at tea parties with opinion being divided. "Just think. Our small colony would be a world leader if women were given the vote."

"I think politics is a man's world. Women have too many more important matters to deal with."

It was some time since Francis had heard news of his father who had now reached the great age of 84. Sadly, his mother Barbara had died three years earlier, and Francis Worrell was now living in Auckland with Walter and his family.

"I hope poor Walter and Emily are not finding my father too much of a trial. Since my mother's death he seems to be even more obsessed with the postage stamp issue and is even talking about returning to London to pursue his claim.”

“Surely he wouldn’t make such a long journey at his age, and where would he stay if he went there? London will be greatly changed since we lived there.”

“His sister Marion is still alive as far as I know and my sisters are living close by. If not, I’m sure that Barbara’s family would welcome him.”

Ellen continued to worry about the situation. Emily was not in good health, burdened down with the grief of losing two teenage children in the past few years.

“It was bad enough when young Caroline was taken, but to lose their lovely son from an accident just three years later was a vicious blow.”

Francis agreed. The death of Caroline had been a huge loss to the family. A bright young woman, studying to become a pupil teacher, she had been overcome by what was termed as ‘brain fever’. For two days before she died, her mind was wandering and her last moments were occupied with totting up figures.

“It was so sad that the two doctors who attended her could do nothing and they put her death down to the mental strain of her examinations.” Her funeral had been held in Auckland where Walter now ran a real estate business, but Francis had been unable to attend, due to pressure of work.

“Thank goodness that their first son Charles is a strong, healthy young man and a successful lawyer. Still interested in the game of cricket, I believe.” Ellen enjoyed hearing news from Emily, whom she missed greatly since the family’s move back to Auckland.

As Francis and Ellen were discussing his fate, Francis Worrell Stevens was, indeed, preparing to travel to England for the first time in more than 30 years. Walter and Emily had done their best to dissuade him, but he knew that he would not rest easily in his grave if he did not present his petition one more time.

He had gained the interest of the Marquis of Carmarthen, George Osborne, who had promised to present the petition in the House of Commons on his behalf.

Apart from his British peerage, George Osborne was MP for Brixton, where Francis was headed, to stay with members of his wife's family. Once he made up his mind, all the arrangements fell smoothly into place.

Without his beloved wife, Francis had lost interest in life in New Zealand. Barbara had died peacefully and was buried in Grafton. The newspaper announcement had read: 'Stevens -in Grey Street Auckland, Barbara, the beloved wife of Francis Worrell Stevens (aged 84) sister of Mr Samuel Vickers of Auckland and the late Charles Vickers of Wormstall Newbury Berks, England. A devoted wife of 56 years.'

With his bags packed and all the paperwork done, Francis was filled with excitement. As well as staying with the family at Brixton, he was planning to return to Loughton to view his old school at Albion Hill. That would bring back memories of his happy days there with Barbara and their young family.

Barbara's brother Samuel Vickers, who was now one of the oldest residents of Auckland, also came to say goodbye. "I would dearly love to accompany you, my friend. We had many good times in the old country and I would have enjoyed meeting my brother's family."

"Take care, Samuel. I may not make the journey back to this country, but I will die happy if the Parliament accepts my petition." It was a sad parting, as Samuel Vickers had been instrumental in bringing the Stevens family to New Zealand so many years ago, and he had the feeling they would not meet again.

Francis had managed to secure a two-berth cabin and as the ship was returning to London with a small number of passengers he was hopeful that he would have the cabin to himself.

There would be no problems with over-crowding as there were very few steerage passengers. His ship was leaving from Dunedin, before calling at Auckland, and the hold would be carrying a shipment of frozen mutton destined for the English market.

As the ship pulled away from the wharf in Auckland, Francis took in the busy scene. The town had expanded onto reclaimed land with huge warehouses and an ornate customs office dominating the waterfront. Small ferries were carrying passengers to the North Shore where he had once owned considerable property.

The tug escorted the ship between the islands and out into the open sea. Once clear of the land, the engines would be shut down and the sails hoisted. New Zealand had treated his family well but now it was time to return home.

Chapter 19

With her wedding day just months away, Clara was anxious to return to Auckland where she could catch up with her mother's family who were organizing the big event. It was to be held in the tiny church at Mauku, near where she spent her early childhood and William's family was hoping to be part of it.

They would ride from Raglan along the coast to Port Waikato and then swim their horses across the Waikato River. It was then a relatively short ride to Mauku along an old military trail.

It was several weeks since Clara had seen her betrothed, but messages were being exchanged by telegraph and post which was aggravatingly slow.

"If only the railway went right through to Auckland, it would be no problem. At this stage the line goes to New Plymouth and then you can take the steamer up the coast to Raglan. I think I will try that route the next time I visit."

"You are right, my dear. The mountainous terrain in the centre of the country has proved too difficult to conquer." Francis was well aware of the time it took to traverse the colony, even though the distance was not great. Shipping still held the advantage over land transport.

"I will call at Uncle Walter's house next time I am in Auckland and hopefully they will be able to come to my wedding. I do hope you and Ellen will also be there."

Francis wasn't so sure. It was years since they had undertaken the long journey to the northern town and he wasn't sure if they would make it. "We'll do our best to be there. Never fear."

"I need to be back in Auckland in the next few weeks, so our wedding plans can be finalized, but I would like to try the rail route to New Plymouth and then the short boat trip up the coast. I could surprise William by landing in Raglan."

Clara set about finalizing her plans and a week later she was dropped off at the railway station for the first phase of her journey. Two steam engines pulled the carriages and the train took off with a hiss and a roar. The wooden seats were hard and she had brought a cushion along to make herself more comfortable.

Soon the town was left behind as they jolted along the narrow line which ran alongside the coast for several miles. Salt spray covered the windows as the waves crashed against the rocks along the shore.

The route then meandered through scattered farms and many miles of dense bush until it reached the town of Wanganui where the railway line crossed a wide river. Clara looked down at the dark water below as the train rolled across the high bridge. She closed her eyes for a moment as her stomach lurched with fear.

Someone opened a window and the carriage was filled with acrid smoke and the clatter of wheels on the rails sounded extra loud. As the train pulled into the station, she was glad to alight from the train to buy a cup of tea and a sandwich at the tearooms.

She stood nervously in the line, hoping the train would not move off without her. A young man standing behind her smiled and said: "Never fear. The guard will give us plenty of warning." Sure enough she was back in her seat clutching the thick white cup and saucer before the whistle was blown and the train continued on its journey.

After a number of quick stops at isolated settlements, the train arrived at New Plymouth where Clara alighted and waited for her luggage which was in the guard's van.

"Where are you heading?" the guard asked and offered to wheel her bag over to a waiting cab.

"Thank you, but I'm only going as far as the station hotel which is just across the street. I won't need a cab as it's just a short walk." Clara was tired but excited at the prospect of being reunited with William. She still had to endure the short steamer ride to Raglan and would need to be at the wharf early in the morning.

She lay awake in the narrow bed that night thinking about William and wondering what he would say when she turned up unannounced in Raglan. It was a very small town and the idea of an unmarried woman arriving at the house of a single man could create a great deal of interest.

"He has been married and has three children. He may not think that I am experienced enough for him." She tossed nervously on the bed and was pleased when morning came and she could board the steamer for the final leg of her journey.

The notoriously rough passage was unusually calm and Clara reached her destination in fine shape. As the ship battled through the rugged surf and anchored safely in Raglan Harbour she breathed a sigh of relief. She would contact William and let him know that she had arrived.

She looked around and was happy at what she saw. Her life of luxury in Oriental Bay was a world away and she was ready to take on a new life and a new challenge.

Walter Stevens was barely out of bed when there was a loud knock on the front door of his home. "Telegraph sir," the boy stated as he thrust a paper into Walter's hand. Walter took the message into the living room where the light was better.

"What is it, my dear." Emily looked on in consternation as Walter unfolded the message. He sat down on the nearest chair and looked across at his wife.

"It is not good news. My father has died in London and has been interred at Lambeth. He was only there for such a short time and was hoping for a good result from the Parliament."

"I am so sorry, but I'm sure your father died knowing he had done his best to have his name associated with the invention of the postage stamp. I only hope that some time in the future, there will be a form of recognition for his idea."

Walter pulled himself together. His wife was right. Francis Worrell Stevens would one day be recognized for the genius he was. "It seems that the family has taken care of the burial details. He died at Mayall Road at the grand age of 85."

Walter wasted no time in relaying the news to Francis in Wellington, and Sydney who was currently working in Dunedin. Sydney's career with the postal service had taken him to many towns and it had been a long time since the brothers had caught up.

"I will arrange with father's solicitor to wind up his estate, though I doubt there will be anything left in his bank accounts." Walter found it was easier to busy himself than to mourn his father. He would remember him as a vital and innovative man who had lived an interesting life with the woman he adored.

He mounted his horse and rode into the town scarcely noticing anything around him. There had been too much sadness over recent years and his mind and soul were cluttered with it. Hopefully, there would be many joyful days to come.

Arriving at the wharf in Raglan was all very well, but how would she contact William to let him know that she was here? What seemed like a good idea at the time didn't feel so great right now. It was almost evening and the place was practically deserted.

Clara looked nervously around and noticed a public house across the street which looked very welcoming. She picked up her bag, which thankfully wasn't too heavy and made her way along the roughly paved road.

A bell rang loudly as she entered the building but there was no-one in sight so she ventured further inside and found herself in the main bar which was filled with burly males. There was a moment's silence as she stood still, wondering what to do.

"Well, hullo bonny lassie. And to what do we owe this pleasure?" A rotund figure with a jovial smile was standing behind the bar, pouring a tankard.

"I have come to see the man I'm engaged to, but I failed to let him know that I was on my way."

"Well then, tell me the name of this lucky gentleman and we will see what we can do." Clara didn't want to spread the word around so she whispered to the bar tender, who laughed and clasped her arm.

"One of our favourite sons. We will dispatch someone to let him know that you are here. In the mean time you must be our guest at dinner where you will be made most welcome."

Clara was bustled into the dining room, a wood panelled area with round tables and high backed chairs. There were a number of women sitting around one table and they looked up in astonishment at the sight of a stranger.

"Come and join us. You must be tired and hungry as you have obviously had a long journey to get here." A tall woman in a most becoming dress pulled up an extra chair and invited Clara to sit down and join the table.

"That is most kind. Yes, I've just got off the steamer and I must admit it has been a long journey all the way from Wellington." Clara sank onto the chair and took the glass of wine that was offered.

"We meet here regularly while our men enjoy their own company. Are you planning on staying in the town?" The women were curious. It wasn't every day that an attractive young lady strolled into the public house unaccompanied.

"I am to be married in the spring and then I will probably visit the town frequently, even though the farm where I will be living is several miles away." Clara felt brave from the alcohol, especially when someone poured her a second drink.

Someone found an extra plate for Clara and soon she was enjoying a delicious meal of roast meat and vegetables. It had been a long time since breakfast at the New Plymouth hotel. The women were bright and friendly and soon knew the story of her engagement to the young widower.

"You are a very lucky woman. There are many young ladies who hoped that William would look in their direction." The stories flowed about William's first wife dying a short time after the birth of her child, leaving all those little girls without a mother.

"I hope you realise that William's ailing father also lives on the farm. You might find yourself looking after an old man as well." The women poured Clara another glass and she was beginning to relax. If the worst came to the worst she could surely stay in the hotel overnight and catch up with William in the morning.

In fact, that was the way it worked out. William was devastated that he couldn't ride over to meet her until next morning. It would have been a treacherous ride back to the farm in the dark. "I will be most happy to see you tomorrow and bring you out to the farm. My father is here as well as the children and they are all eager to meet you again," he had written.

It was late by the time the women had finished their meal and caught up with their men folk and the jolly party was over for the night. Clara was relieved to be given a comfortable room with a soft bed and wash stand. She was too tired to take advantage of the bath down the corridor and vowed to make use of it after a good night's sleep.

She was sure she would make many good friends in this new town.

Chapter 20

It took Francis some time to digest the news of his father's death. "I knew that he was unlikely to return to New Zealand and I hope his last days were happy ones." He showed the telegraph to Ellen, who sighed deeply.

"I'm sure we will hear from the family in London. They will know the result of his quest with the Parliament. It seems he was destined to be buried in a simple plot in Lambeth, while Rowland Hill is lying in state at Westminster Abbey."

"There's no denying Sir Rowland's good work with the postal service deserved to be recognized and my father would not have taken that honour from him. He was mostly annoyed about the monument at Kidderminster paid for by the people of the town. I wonder if he ever got to see it."

Ellen smiled. "I would like to have seen the look on his face if he did stand beside the great statue. He would have been protesting loudly to everyone in ear shot."

Francis knew there was little they could do for his father now. It would have been good to see him buried with his wife at Grafton in Auckland, but that was not to be. Hopefully they were now reunited in the next world.

With the major elections coming up later in the year Francis was as busy as ever. There were high hopes that the new Liberal Party would be elected as this could lead to major reforms throughout the country. Urgent work was needed to establish a consistent roading and rail network.

The Hay Street properties were keeping Ellen busy. One of the larger houses was still being run as a boarding house and Ellen was often in conflict with the rather flamboyant woman who ran the establishment. One case, concerning an argument over payment of rent, was heard by the court and a jury of 12 which ruled in favour of Ellen Stevens. However, the case was a topic of conversation around the town for some time.

"Young women are beginning to talk at tea parties, saying there is trouble with their land lady. I'm very unhappy to have such gossip being spread about me. I've always considered myself to be a fair and honest woman." Ellen was most annoyed at having her good name compromised.

William had completed his schooling and a position was organised for him in the Government building. His good record had earned him the chance to work as a clerk and he was happy to follow in his father's footsteps.

He rode proudly off with Francis each morning while John waited for the horse-drawn tram which would take him to school. He was proving to be a top scholar and had been offered an apprenticeship in a lawyers' office when his final year was completed.

"There is so much work for a solicitor when it comes to settling land claims. I would find that very challenging," he said.

Ellen was very impressed to think that John may one day become a lawyer. That was a very prestigious position. John was also a keen football player and followed his father's interest in rifle shooting.

Ellen's many interests kept her busy but she still found the time to swim each day at the beach in front of her house during the summer. She would wrap herself in a loose gown over her bathing costume and carry a large towel which she placed on the sand. She always carried a colourful sunshade to protect her fine skin and wore a bathing cap over her braided hair. At times she would meet a friend and they would sit and chat for a time.

She always took her turn to provide afternoon tea for the Bridge Club and had become quite an expert player.

There had been good news from Sydney and his wife. They had been married for more than 10 years without being blessed with a child and now Annie was at long last pregnant and due around the same time as Clara's wedding date.

"Annie is not a young woman, so I hope everything goes well. It would be such a joy for them to have a healthy child." Ellen was not so sure that she would want a child so late in life, but wished her sister-in-law well.

"September promises to be a very exciting month with Clara's wedding and a child for Annie and Sydney. It will make up for all the sad times we have lived through." Francis was almost as confident as Ellen about the future of their family.

Ellen had also befriended a woman named Kate Sheppard who was promoting the petition calling for Parliament to allow votes for women. Being a keen businesswoman herself, Ellen, like Clara, was very much drawn to the cause.

"Why should men have all the say? Women have just as much right to choose the government," she said to Francis one evening. "I will support this woman and help collect names for the petition."

"I'm sure you will my dear. And I know the new Parliament is likely to allow women to vote at the next election." Francis saw no reason why women shouldn't be allowed to help choose the government.

When Clara woke in a hotel bedroom in Raglan she was at first startled by the strange surroundings. She had slept soundly after her pleasant evening but felt a little nervous about meeting William again.

The smell of fried bacon wafted up the stairs and she roused herself and made her way to the bathroom. Fortunately, it was unoccupied so she locked the door and ran the water into the deep bathtub. It was a great relief to soak in the warm water after the long journey and Clara soon relaxed and felt ready for the day ahead.

Luckily she had brought a light bag which could easily be carried on horseback. She knew that William would bring an extra horse for the ride back to the farm.

She was enjoying a tasty breakfast when a familiar voice sounded in the outer office. Her heart jumped when William entered the room, looking so handsome with his thick curly hair and tanned skin. She rose from her chair and was soon in his arms.

"This is such a pleasant surprise. Everyone back on the farm is eagerly waiting to see you again." William held Clara at arm's length to look at her. He could hardly believe that she was here and they would be together once more.

"I look forward to meeting your family and I do so want to see the farm where I will be living. I hope you don't mind me just turning up like this." Clara blushed as William's arms tightened around her. She had no doubt that this was where she wanted to be.

As William had left home early he was persuaded to join Clara and soon a plate of bacon, eggs and warm toast was placed before him. They ate companionably in silence for a time then William explained that there would be no problem with Clara staying in his home.

"The three little girls are living with their grandparents at present but my father will be there to chaperone us." William laughed. "He is quite deaf and almost blind but your reputation will remain unsullied."

William paid the landlord for the night's accommodation while Clara packed her bag and soon they were saddled up and heading for the Kauroa Valley which was about an hour's ride away.

As they climbed the steep terrain Clara looked back and took in the expanse of the Raglan Harbour and the line of breakers which pounded onto the coast. At first they followed a clay road but soon the track became narrower. The bush grew thicker here with giant fern and clumps of flax mingling with a wide variety of native trees.

"The farm does seem to be rather isolated. Does anyone else live near here?" Clara was beginning to feel nervous. They were now a long way from civilization.

"Wait until we reach the valley and you will see a number of farm houses. We have a very friendly community there and everyone wants to meet you." William could understand Clara's apprehension. The track from Raglan was a primitive one, but the valley was now attracting many people on the look out for suitable properties.

William was right. When they reached the top of the ridge they stopped their horses and looked across the vista of the valley. Patches of bush remained but much of the land had been cleared and sheep and cattle grazed on the new grassland with settlers' cottages dotting the landscape.

"It is quite beautiful; a little like Mauku where the wedding will be held." Clara felt happier now there was evidence of habitation. "How much longer before we reach the farm?"

"We are almost there and the children are staying a short distance away. I do hope you will be happy here. My poor wife was content enough but suffered from ill health through her last pregnancy. She died just three weeks after the child was born and the place is definitely missing a feminine touch."

William was worried that the house might not be up to Clara's standards. He had heard of her life in Wellington, living in a grand residence with maids doing all the hard work. Her cousins had warned him, but now she was here to see the conditions for herself.

The horses were weary, but knowing they were close to home trotted eagerly along the grassy track. Soon a large farm house came into view, a long verandah across the front. A rough wooden fence separated the house site from the fields beyond but the grass needed cutting and the garden was completely overgrown.

"As I said, the place has been missing the feminine touch but it is sound and could be made very comfortable." Clara took one look at William's despondent face and smiled. "Don't worry. It looks fine to me. I can see myself sitting on that verandah waiting for you to come in for dinner." She dismounted and led her horse to the gate.

William took the horses and unsaddled them, then let them free in the field to graze. He held out his hand to Clara. "Come, my dear. Let me show you my humble dwelling."

Chapter 21

The closer the date came for Clara's wedding the more Ellen longed to be there. Although she had travelled over the South Island she had never made the journey north and she was keen to visit Auckland and catch up with Walter and Emily.

"We really must be there for Clara. She has been such a good daughter to us and I do so want to meet her new family."

"I agree. It would be a most pleasant event and I am due to have time off. We will make the arrangements immediately." Francis could see no reason not to travel to Auckland, even though it involved an uncomfortable steamer journey up the coast.

They would stay in Auckland with Walter and Emily and travel by a small boat from Onehunga to Waiuku. "I believe the Kentish Hotel in Waiuku offers accommodation. From there it is a short journey to the Mauku church where the ceremony will be held." Francis was reading a travel page and planning their journey. He was looking forward to returning to the area where he had lived during his time in the militia. It would be strange to go back to the little church where he and Maria had been married all those years ago.

"I wish to give Clara and William a full set of linen, but we can buy that when we get to Auckland rather than take it with us on the boat, and we will contribute towards the wedding feast." Ellen was always most generous when it came to weddings.

Over the next few days Ellen was busy sending telegraphs off to confirm the arrangements. Clara's wedding would be the highlight of the year.

Clara spent three glorious days staying at William's home. His elderly father was a quiet old gentleman who sat smoking his pipe out on the verandah most of the day. As long as he was given a meal three times a day he was content.

The visit to meet the three children was a little more daunting. William's mother-in-law had taken them in when her daughter died and although she enjoyed their company, she would be pleased to see a younger woman take over the role.

The eldest girl looked at Clara with suspicion while the two younger ones were more talkative. They were thrilled to see their father and outdid each other to gain his attention. After an hour or two, Clara was quite exhausted even though she had grown up with her younger siblings back in Wellington.

She said nothing to William, not wanting to spoil their precious time together. "I would like to ride over the farm today," she said on the last day of the visit. "I will make us a picnic and we can find a peaceful spot to enjoy it."

William agreed. He would be sad to see Clara leave on the boat in the morning and wanted to make the most of the time that was left. "That sounds like a great idea. Father can find himself some bread and cheese for lunch and I will show you the grand estate."

The farm had been virgin bush land when William's father first arrived but much of it had now been cleared and fenced into fields. A well worn track wound up to the top of the ridge from where the ocean could be seen sparkling in the distance.

"Just think. I will be out there tomorrow. I hope it is a calm trip." Clara was not looking forward to the journey. Although the distance was not great, the west coast could be treacherous and the boat would need to cross the infamous bar to enter the Manukau Harbour.

"I probably won't see you again until our wedding day. I will work on the house and have it ready for you to come back to after we have honeymooned in Auckland. I know you will make me very happy."

They dismounted and Clara found herself in William's arms. He held her tightly, then let her go and busied himself, unpacking the picnic and laying a rug over the rough ground. "Sit yourself down. We will eat our lunch and save our love making until we are wed, although I am sorely tempted."

"We've waited this long. We can wait a little longer. Soon we will be together for ever."

Clara sighed with happiness. Her love for William had grown even stronger over the past few days and their wedding day couldn't come quickly enough. She had already met a number of the neighbours and a big bonus was that her Aunt Emilia and numerous cousins lived a short distance away.

Back at her grandparents' home there would be plenty to do to keep her occupied. She was sad that she would not be returning to Wellington where she had lived happily for so many years.

"I hope my father and Ellen will be able to make the journey for the wedding. It would be so special if they could be there."

The day passed happily and William held Clara in his arms that evening as they watched the sun set over the distant hills. Tomorrow they would ride to the wharf where the steamer would be waiting.

There was a new air of excitement in Wellington as the general election was to be held later in the year. It was predicted that the Liberal candidate John Ballance would give Harry Atkinson, the current leader, a run for his money.

There had been many improvements to the town's water supply and electricity was beginning to replace gas lighting on the streets.

"I think that technology will change the way we live in the next few years. We may be driving around in petrol-powered vehicles and the trams will be run by electricity." Francis could hardly take in the changes that were occurring before their eyes. "We just need to construct a better drainage system and Wellington would be a very pleasant place to live. Too many people are dying from diseases that could be prevented."

"The proposed scheme is very costly and people don't think they can afford to pay more rates. I know that most of the councillors are opposed to it. However, I wouldn't want to be living in the parts of town that have sewage-soaked back yards." Ellen was pleased to see progress but hoped the residents could afford to pay higher rates.

She had received favourable replies from Walter and Emily who were more than happy to accommodate them.

They would all spend the night at the Kentish Hotel before taking a small boat to Mauku for the big event.

"I'm disappointed that we won't be seeing Clara until her wedding day. I would love to have taken her shopping for a wedding gown, but her ideas would probably be very different from mine." Ellen missed the excitement of being part of the big celebration. She would dearly love to have held the reception in their spacious home at Oriental Bay where Frank's reception had been such a success.

"Clara will have plenty of support from her family at Mauku. I believe the whole village has been invited to the wedding." Francis recalled the day that he and his first wife had been married in a double ceremony along with Maria's brother. It seemed a lifetime away.

His parents had been there as well as Barbara's brother Samuel, who was still alive and well in Auckland. Hopefully he too would be able to attend the ceremony in the old church that he had helped establish.

Chapter 22

The small white church on the hill stood out like a beacon, the simple cross silhouetted against the cloudless blue sky, as Francis drove the pony and carriage through the narrow gateway. His daughter Clara looked charming in the cream satin gown which moulded her slim figure. A lace veil was secured by a garland of cream roses and she would carry a simple floral bouquet into the church.

The two bridesmaids were already waiting near the steps, wearing identical lace dresses in soft dusky pink. The organ music could be heard as Francis helped Clara down from the cart and the horse was led away.

William and his two attendants were standing nervously in the church. On a signal from the usher, the organ tone changed to the traditional bridal march and all heads were turned as the bride and her father walked slowly up the aisle.

Clara took in the crowded church, but her eyes were fixed firmly on her husband-to-be who looked so handsome in the borrowed suit. A crisp white shirt and black bow tie sat rather awkwardly on his tall frame but a huge smile lit up his face.

William had known sad times and endured three lonely years but today would change everything. Clara would be his wife and his soul mate.

Ellen sat upright in the front row and Francis turned and sat beside her. She took his arm and gave him a squeeze of affection. Clara had grown up in their home, from a child to a handsome young woman and today she looked so happy.

They had spent a comfortable night at the Kentish Hotel, enjoying good country hospitality and a lavish meal. The host had supplied a fine dish of roasted pheasant along with platefuls of vegetables fresh from the local gardens.

This morning when the tide was full they had boarded a small craft which took them all the way up a narrow inlet to the landing place near Mauku and from there it was just a short cart ride to the settlement and church.

Ellen turned and smiled at Emily who sat beside Walter in the second row. The two women were dressed in the most elaborate gowns with ornate gold jewellery and large feathered hats, which set them apart from the country folk in their more sedate clothing.

Emily was pleased that her niece was marrying such a fine man, but tears came to her eyes as she remembered her daughter and her untimely death just five years previously. It should have been Caroline walking down the aisle today she thought sadly.

Walter must have known what she was thinking as he took her hand and held it firmly. Nothing was going to be allowed to spoil this wonderful occasion. He was enjoying the company of his brother and Ellen who had been staying at their home in Auckland for the past few days. They planned to be there for another week before returning to Wellington on the steamer.

Samuel Vickers sat proudly in the middle of the church which he had helped establish so many years ago. He remembered how proud the early settlers had been when the church was opened and how, a short time later, it was used as a garrison when the Maori uprisings had threatened the newcomers.

"If it hadn't been for me, Francis Worrell and my sister would never have brought their family to this country," he thought. "We would not be here today celebrating this wedding."

He had lived for 91 long years and hoped for a few more to come. He looked around at his former neighbours who had stayed in the district to improve their farms. He had moved and prospered in the city and his family had contributed much to the growth of this young country. What would the next 90 years bring for this promising new land?

Author's note

Whenever I visit Wellington, I walk along Oriental Parade and stop at the old band rotunda from where I can see Hay Street and the gracious villas which have stood the test of time.

I watch the people enjoying the beautiful beach, such a short walk from the city centre, and imagine my great grandfather, Francis Stevens, and his wife Ellen sitting outside their property, collecting signatures which saved the beach from becoming a boat slip.

I look past the high rise on the corner, to the houses which Ellen had built and where they lived their busy lives.

I have made a few changes to this edition of the book as I have found out more facts about the Stevens family, including the cause of Maria Stevens and her young daughter's deaths and the subdivision named Laketown on Auckland's North Shore.

After Ellen Stevens died from a heart attack on the beach in 1916, the properties were left to several members of her family. Unfortunately, we don't own any of them now. My grandfather John Stevens was still living in Number 10 until his death in 1960 and it was there that my mother grew up and I spent many a happy family holiday.

As for Francis Worrell Stevens, I wish I had known his story as I was growing up. He must have been an extremely interesting character, always thinking of fresh ideas but not often carrying them out.

Over the years there have been several claims made about the origin of the postage stamp and I believe that Francis Worrell Stevens thought of the idea as he claimed, but didn't follow it through.

His name has been recently recognised, however, on one of a series of blue heritage plaques in Loughton, Essex outside the Hollies, 11 Albion Hill. It says: 'Sir Rowland Hill and Francis Worrell Stevens, who were pioneers of the postage stamp, lived here.'